DISCARD

The Devil's Jury

A Mystery Novel

D.S. KAPLAN

ISBN: 978-1-4834-6017-8 (sc)
ISBN: 978-1-4834-6016-1 (e)

Because of the dynamic nature of the Internet, any web addresses or links contained in this book may have changed since publication and may no longer be valid. The views expressed in this work are solely those of the author and do not necessarily reflect the views of the publisher, and the publisher hereby disclaims any responsibility for them.

Any people depicted in stock imagery provided by Thinkstock are models, and such images are being used for illustrative purposes only.
Certain stock imagery © Thinkstock.

Lulu Publishing Services rev. date: 10/21/2016

To My Wife Lyn
Our Kids
and Their Kids

Contents

Foreword

Veniremen

A jury is impaneled from eligible participants who are supposed to represent common citizens. In the judicial process, these "nominees" are called veniremen although it would seem more politically correct to call them "venire people", persons or human beings. But to avoid such manslaughter of the language, let's keep it to its original—veniremen. It derives from the British practice of sending notices to compel citizens to report for jury service—venire facias—to be made to come—which of course derives from Latin.

Most Americans know what it really means. You receive a notice in the mail. You groan when you see that it comes from the courthouse. You groan louder when you see that it's for an extremely inconvenient date. (Of course, there is no good time, if you are involved with living your life.) You quickly consider claiming a fatal disease, taking a long vacation, changing your name, etc. Then you see that the penalties for shirking your responsibility range from name calling to horrible sounding judicial remedies. And you serve.

Serving on less legal or formal groups can be much more interesting. At least until the first murder.

Jury Duty

They had been meeting so often and for so long that the group had a acquired a name—The Devil's Jury. No one could clearly remember how or why the name evolved. It had just become easier to refer to it by a name. "Will I see you at DJ tonight?" "Who was at the Devil's Jury the other night?"

The members weren't sure whether the name or the DJ acronym had come first. What did it mean? Hard to say. Was it because they passed judgment on almost everything? When the bar's proprietor, a former teacher named Michael Nielsen, mentioned that The Inquisition had been referred to as "God's Jury", they decided to give the devil his due. They criticized celebrities, the government, neighbors, and of course, politicians.

Bar None was a nice neighborhood bar designed for hanging out, but its impact was felt far beyond the neighborhood. Posters, signs, graphics and photos all over the place, leaving no visible wall. It was essentially one big open space—tables, chairs, and bar stools scattered to allow intimate conversation. Almost everyone could see, but not necessarily hear, everybody else—be seen and not heard. An ordinary place with a sometimes extraordinary effect.

The group was seated at its traditional table—a large round table furthest from the long and often crowded bar. The regulars were all there, Keith, Larry, Dan, Sheryl and Ben Freeman and three sometime attendees—referred to disparagingly in the group's jury parlance as alternates.

The number of "jurors" on a given night could be as high as a dozen. More often it was six or eight. Like any jury (or social drinking group), the DJ was anything but exclusive. It was almost universal—not only with respect to age, color and social class but also with regard to gender.

The conversations varied from night to night. Several factors contributed to the longevity of this group. Above all, there was a mutual respect and a genuine fondness among the "jurors". They all enjoyed the time they spent away from work. They liked each other, and appreciated the banter that occasionally morphed into genuine discussion. They talked about the three topics forbidden in most groups of acquaintances— religion (not a lot), politics (a lot), and sex (usually as an undercurrent). In addition, most of them took stabs at amateur criticism of the basics— movies, food, celebrities, TV, trivia, and music. Not in that order. There was no fixed time or day for meeting, but the patrons and staff of the bar were used to the Jury congregating and, in fact, most of those around them appreciated the conviviality and spirit that radiated from the group.

One sure-fire way to stimulate discussion with the Jury was to initiate a bitch session. The group could bitch about anything. When several members had arrived late, the discussion turned to the nearby construction site that had delayed them and had been a thorn in the side of nearby businesses and residents. "It took me twice as long to get here," said Keith Gallon.

The Devil's Jurors took seats and greeted each other as they had dozens of times before. They conversed and drank freely. Tonight the variety of beverages was as selective as a Reader's Digest Sweepstakes— all types of drinks were represented—beers, whiskey, tequila shots, a Cosmopolitan, and even a martini. Of course, Dan Daniels had his signature shot of Jack Daniel's.

The martini belonged to Ben Freeman. Ben was a very tall, mostly bald and extremely thin accountant. He was so thin that he could roll his stomach on command like a wave, and you could actually hear the water swishing around in it. As he performed that feat with beer, he said "The traffic was backed up like trucks in a row." He was noted for mixing metaphors which the group referred to as "BenFrees"—his mismatches and combinations of clichés were uniquely his own—funny and usually unintentionally so.

"Big deal," responded Keith's brother Larry, "your whole trip is only twenty-five minutes. I have to pass that damn site almost every day."

Sheryl Common chimed in, "I do too."

Dan said, "They don't do a lot of work either, mostly just sit around and drink coffee and eat donuts." Dan Daniels was on old friend of the brothers and Sheryl. "In fact you two Gallons moved to our beautiful and quaint North Shore and brought the damn traffic with you."

"What do you mean?" protested Keith and Larry in unison—it might have even been in harmony.

"I mean that the town that spawned you two, Framingham, has more cars, asphalt, restaurants, malls, and stores per square mile than anywhere on the East Coast." An exaggeration to be sure but it was an apt description. Dan paused for effect and added, "Including Manhattan!"

Ben ventured, "Yeh, they're all gold-bedding and feather bricking." The group exchanged glances acknowledging the second BenFree of the evening. Another member said, "My dad used to operate a backhoe and follow up with a shovel. He'd come home filthy, exhausted and stinking of asphalt."

Dan jumped in, "Most blondes think that asphalt is a rectal disease." A couple of jurors raised their glasses to toast the night's first and probably worst play on words.

Sheryl got a little serious. "It's frustrating that we can't do anything about these slackers making it tough for us to get anywhere. I'm thankful that I only have to hear the noise when I drive by. I'd hate to have to listen all day."

For the next forty five minutes, the Jury deliberated on government excesses and corruption, and got themselves pretty well worked up. It wasn't a group to be polite—or even very tolerant—of boredom. Once the yawns started, they had about fifteen minutes before they adjourned.

Dan customarily made a comment or joke to conclude the evening. Tonight was no exception. "I watched the other day and there were two guys walking around a construction site. One would dig a hole and then the other would fill it back up."

That didn't seem to make sense on any level.

Dan waited and then explained, "They said there were supposed to be three of them and one would dig, the second would install posts and the third would fill it up. The second guy was out sick."

They realized that they had been "had" again by Dan, and took the cue to leave.

The Devil's Jury had reached a verdict. The construction crew was guilty—of something. Most of the members were unaware that in a matter of days a death sentence would be carried out.

Sheith

As they often did, Sheryl and Keith left Bar None together. Some nights they were joined by Larry and some nights Keith would stay to work his part time job at the Bar. But mostly it was Keith and Sheryl. Some of the jurors thought that it was romance that brought Keith and Sheryl together. They would be surprised that it was Keith's brother that introduced them.

Larry Gallon and Sheryl Common met through work. Larry had parlayed business and art courses into a marketing career. Over the years, he worked as a creative artist and director with several advertising agencies and worked independently as well. Being a creative type, Larry sported a flair for flamboyance. He almost always wore a fedora from his collection of wild colors, appropriate for supporting his swashbuckling style. He specialized in creating and writing advertising and publicity campaigns.

Sheryl, on the other hand, was more nuts and bolts, efficiently arranging events, functions, news conferences and, occasionally managing crisis communications for clients. She called her practice Common Ground. Sheryl and Larry got along well and when it made sense, they collaborated.

On one such occasion, Larry brought Sheryl in to help his longstanding client with the communications strategy and plan the company's 20th anniversary event. Larry doffed his blue fedora as he and Sheryl sat down in his client's office to review the year's strategy and budget.

As the client listed the projects and expenses, he mentioned that he was having his website updated.

He was three items further down on the list when Larry interrupted and said, "Sam, could you repeat that?"

"Repeat what?"

"The part about the website."

"We've budgeted for enhancements to the website," the client said.

"What am I, chopped liver?" Larry asked.

"Larry, what are you talking about?"

"I'm your friend, we've been working together for years, and you hire someone else to work on the website?!"

"I didn't know...."

Larry flew out of his chair and began to flail about, wildly roaring a stream of rhetoric, "You didn't know that I do websites? You hired someone else? A stranger? Do I do websites?" Do politicians lie? Do I do websites?" He flung himself on the floor. Prostrate, he pleaded, "Sam, here. Walk all over me. Stomp out my hopes and dreams, my professional dignity."

Exhausted, Larry lay flat on the floor and closed his eyes. Sam looked at Sheryl for some understanding. She tried to look impassive, inscrutable.

Finally, the client sighed. "OK, Larry."

Larry looked up, hopeful.

"All right Larry. That was quite a performance. Do you really do websites?"

"Do I do websites? Does a telemarketer always call at the worst time? Does a golfer cheat?"

"OK, I haven't signed a contract with this guy. It's yours if you want it."

"I want it. I'll call you tomorrow." Larry calmed down and they finished the agenda and concluded the meeting.

A few minutes later, as Sheryl pressed the elevator button for the first floor, she said, "Wow, I didn't know you did websites either." They entered the elevator.

Larry put his hat on with a flourish. He grinned, "How hard could it be?"

———∿∿⚬∾⚬✕⚬⚬✕∾⚬∿∿———

As much as Sheryl Common hated to admit it to herself, she always had one eye peeled for relationship potential. She worked in public relations and most of her co-workers were young, attractive, bright, and ambitious females—a very competitive market. The few males in the profession were usually older, and often married.

She still managed to date, either getting fixed up or occasionally dating someone she met through friends or at work. In two separate instances, Sheryl almost found Mr. Right. One turned out to be Mr. Left and the other turned out to be Mr. Wrong. Mr. Left was a nice guy. An engineer. Sometimes a little too serious. At other times a little too weird. Always nice, not always considerate. Almost everything distracted him. She had to work her way up to discussing anything intimate with him. She had two obstacles to overcome—getting his attention and then, breaking down his inhibitions to focus on something he usually overlooked—his feelings.

Once he stopped in the midst of an intimate discussion of their sexual pasts and their erotic futures to mention a new software application that could really help her with her work. Sheryl rolled her eyes heavenward, "You could be on your way to an all-expense paid cruise around the world with Jennifer Lawrence, and if someone offered you a new computer gizmo, you'd jump ship to get it."

When she told Larry about this, he shook his head, "the poor bastard has his head in the clouds or in cyberspace—or up his ass. He doesn't appreciate you, Sheryl." A month or two later the relationship with Mr. Left collapsed. That conversation with Larry was probably the critical crack in the foundation. Larry was unaware that he had had such an impact on Sheryl's romantic life.

He did it again. Unintentionally. When he and Sheryl were having drinks a friend of his stopped by. Larry introduced Sheryl to him, "Sheryl, this is Dan Daniels, my brother from another mother." Dan had welcomed the Gallon brothers to the North Shore and been so close that he was like family.

Sheryl stared. He was beyond good-looking; he was movie star good-looking. Drop Dead handsome. Bronze-blond hair, his nose and chin were the perfect fit for his face. He had unblinking, glittering ice blue eyes, and a dimpled cheek to make his visage distinctive. His one jagged tooth was the single imperfection that somehow made his appearance more palatable.

Dan smiled, "Hi, Sheryl."

Sheryl shook his hand, smiled, and said unnecessarily, "Hi, my name is Sheryl."

Dan Daniels turned out to be Mr. Wrong.

He had too many stereotypical Irish-American traits for his own good. He was a raconteur and ringleader of sorts. He drank Jack Daniel's and always got laughs. He related stories, used puns and dirty jokes, and made ribald, corny, or provocative comments.

He could charm, confuse, or cajole on command. Especially when he was drinking.

And drink he did. He always seemed to have a drink at hand. Although most of his friends rarely observed him actually drinking, they all could picture him, drink in hand, relating a story or retelling a joke. He ordered and reordered, but rarely got drunk. He kept small bottles of Jack Daniel's at all of his close friends' homes. His first or second sentence upon entering would be "How about some Jack for Daniels?"

She couldn't remember having so much fun or excitement in her life. Sheryl would sometimes wonder how Dan could maintain his work schedule with such a demanding social (drinking) schedule. When he was let go from an IT job at a professional service firm, he was upset for a while, but rebounded. He stayed out at bars most nights but seemed to have found his niche as a freelance geek for an IT company. His attitude fluctuated from enjoying the challenge of finding a problem and fixing it to one of rote distraction. Either way, it was the perfect vocation for him. Maybe the monotonous flat sine wave of the job was the reason that he seemed to be performing or acting out on most nights.

Their romance was intense but brief. Despite the adventurous and entertaining nature of their relationship, she was frequently filled with anxiety, occasionally bordering on terror. Sometimes he would show up an hour or two late for a date— with some outrageous and elaborate story. After a while, he wouldn't give her a reason— just an angry glare. "Some problems are worse than waiting comfortably at home for a few minutes."

Dan was moody, periodically sinking into depression or quaking with anger. When he would speak coherently during these black and blue periods, what he said wasn't pretty. He would be abusive and insulting. He would never hit her, but he would humiliate her. He had maimed her ego on several occasions. Sheryl was a Frances McDormand type. Like many character actors, she could be attractive or glamorous on one day, dowdy the next. Her appearance had a certain chameleon quality and on her off-days her ego was fragile.

When he wanted to, Dan would tap into her deepest doubts and fears. "You know Sheryl, if you don't watch out, you'll wind up alone. You keep treating me this way, and you'll have no one but our crazy friend Keith. And he won't live with you, he won't put up with your bullshit. You'll be a lonely old lady—no husband, no lover, no children, no family—completely alone. So maybe you should treat me better." On other occasions he would ridicule her, "How can you be so stupid? You mean you actually believed them when they told you that you would get that account? Why would they want you?"

Sheryl eventually tired of the harassment. She no longer remained sullen and silent during his abusive tirades. She would argue, cry, or walk out. She could sense that he was losing interest. So was she.

One night she asked him if he was seeing someone else.

"You know how a woman knows when her man is cheating?" he asked.

Sheryl just stared at him, undeterred. Dan continued exuding his patented charm and humor, "When he starts bathing twice a week."

Sheryl stared. Dan persisted, "You haven't noticed me bathing more, have you?" That unsuccessful attempt at deflection was his exit line. He called the following day and Sheryl told him she didn't want to see him again.

She never did. He disappeared from her romantic life.

Months later when they happened to meet at the Devil's Jury, the hard feelings were gone—along with the passion. No one seemed to be aware of their ill-fated affair.

———꒰ɷꙬʘꙬɷ꒱———

When Larry Gallon married Carolyn Johnston, it was kind of a bad news-good news situation for Keith. The bad news was that Larry was no longer as available to spend time with him. The good news was that Keith reveled in Larry's settled life. As the years passed, the marriage grew—two wonderful children, a boy and a girl, a nice house. Keith enjoyed his niece and nephew and it helped fill the vacuum left by his brother's new focus. They all agreed that Keith had found two friends at his level of maturity. He was a big kid and the role of playful uncle suited him perfectly.

Keith visited often to sample the flavor of their blissful domestic routine. Carolyn would cook. Larry would joke about her lack of culinary prowess, always winking at Keith to alert him to prepare to laugh. The kids would play, and Larry and Carolyn seemed impervious to the din. Keith enjoyed his visits, but he would always smile to himself on the way home, newly appreciative of the peace and quiet of bachelorhood. He was content with vicarious domesticity.

In the meantime, Larry and Sheryl had formed a solid working relationship. He appreciated her tolerance and character, and was aware that she was having no luck but bad luck with dates. She was clearly underappreciated by prospective suitors. Larry was very married so he did the next best thing to asking her out. He fixed her up with his brother

Keith. He began his merger plan by inviting both Keith and Sheryl for dinner with him and Carolyn.

For their dinner, the four went to a "nice little Italian restaurant" in Boston's North End. The area was famous primarily for three things—a real European neighborhood atmosphere, delicious Italian food at reasonable prices, and a painful shortage of parking. Larry drove. He and Carolyn searched for parking spaces and bickered as only married couples can. In the back seat Keith and Sheryl bonded via facial reactions to the tumult in the front seat. By the time they parked and walked to the restaurant, Sheryl and Keith knew that they were simpatico without having spoken a lot.

The place was called Firenze Trattoria. It was small and crowded and genuinely pleasant. The host sat them and said that their server would be Anna.

Within a matter of minutes a nice-looking young waitress approached the table. "Hi, my name is Anna and I'll be your server." The group nodded hello. "I'll take your drink orders, but first I have some oral specials—...."

Instantly Larry blurted, "I'll take one."

Keith said, "I'll take two."

There was a brief pause—frozen like a video still frame. Then all four diners burst out laughing. A half second later, the waitress realized how her offer was being interpreted and she started to laugh uncontrollably. She stooped and held onto the table until she could control her laughing. Then she took the group's drink orders and went into the kitchen to place the orders. Ten seconds later the diners were treated to an uproar from the kitchen as Anna repeated the story.

She was pink-faced through every course of what was a delicious dinner. At the end of the night she confessed to the table, "I will never say 'oral specials' again, but I had more fun tonight than I've ever had as a waitress." It was the auspicious beginning of a relationship for Keith and Sheryl.

However, the relationship didn't go as Larry had planned. It wasn't a romance, but it evolved into a close friendship. A marathon drinking bout had cemented their special relationship. She respected his intelligence and enjoyed his humor. She knew he felt the same about her. Keith and Sheryl spent so much time together, that their friends at Bar None took to referring to them as Sheith.

They felt comfortable with each other. Outmoded gender biases disappeared. When called upon, Keith would provide gal-pal companionship. He would shop, gossip, or binge on chocolate with her. He would even go to a five handkerchief tear jerker with her.

Likewise she could be a buddy for him — drink beer and watch sports, tell stupid jokes, recall Three Stooges routines or, when hard pressed, even burp on cue. She gradually came to enjoy screaming and yelling over a hockey game. She surprised herself the first time she found herself hoping that one of the Boston Bruins would pick a fight with one of the visiting players.

Keith and Sheryl just liked each other. It was a relationship no one fully understood. Many of their friends assumed that their friendship was sexual or romantic—or at least contained a sensual element. After all they were unattached and definitely heterosexual. The prevailing wisdom among their friends was, "Where there's smoke, there's fire." In reality, where there was smoke, there was warmth.

Donut Hole

Artie Rollins weaved his way among backhoes, pipes, and other tools of construction and destruction. Silent, they reminded him of metallic dinosaurs, but right now they were obstacles. His co-workers were leaning and talking to each other, already munching on donuts. He hurried over to the excavated pit where his friend Jack was usually "holed up". "Jack, you got any 'healthy' donuts down there?"

He leaned over just as a Dunkin' Donuts box was hoisted in a somewhat chubby, and definitely dirty, hand. Jack "Hammer" Parker stood up, smiled, and patted his incomparable beer-belly, "They're right here."

Artie and announced loud enough for several of his friends to hear, "Hey Jack, I have a riddle."

Jack Parker took a bite of a donut, "OK, I'll bite."

"What's the difference between the Red Sox and a swarm of mosquitoes?"

Jack raised his arms quizzically and looked around at the group on break. He took a another dramatic bite of the donut. "OK, I'll bite again."

Artie spun slowly, engaging his audience. "After a while the mosquitoes stop sucking."

As snickers subsided, Artie calculated the number of donuts being consumed around him. He might be out of luck. Sure enough, as he leaned over Jack's chest-high square hole, a glance told him that the donuts had indeed been decimated. Three and a half remained. He wondered which one of his beefy friends had an appetite so dainty that he restricted himself to half a donut.

"You've got to be quicker, Artie, or you'll starve around here," Jack grinned and held the box out to him. Artie wandered away, biting into a jelly donut. The equipment started up noisily, announcing that break time was over. Artie turned to ask Jack for the first shot at the donuts the next time. Jack's face had once again disappeared from the rim of the pit. Not wanting to shout over the mechanical clamor, Artie retraced his steps and peered over the edge. Jack was lying on the bottom of the pit, with two huge red wounds spreading across his donut-bloated belly.

Artie just stood. He couldn't believe it. It was unreal. Too much like the beginning of a television police procedural. The world actually started to spin. The men, the dust, and the noise overwhelmed him. He couldn't process what was happening. He jumped into the pit, feeling deep down that his friend was beyond help. He held his friend, oblivious to the distinct odor of blood. He was unaware that his friends and co-workers stood around the rim of the pit, staring down dumbfounded at him and his friend. When the police arrived, he was still sitting beside his friend's body, numb. Moaning quietly.

Jack Parker had been shot. The rest of the work day was suspended. The crew waited to be questioned and searched. The area was cordoned off; names were taken, statements given. No weapon was found. As the workers dispersed, no one could begin to understand who or why anyone would want to kill Jack.

Dizzy

The call rudely interrupted her morning tai chi, so Detective Gillespie drove to the crime scene directly from home. A construction worker had been shot and killed at a work site. The area was definitely in transition. She passed by buildings various stages of disrepair and rebuilding. Crumbling foundations destined for the wrecking ball alternated with new solid bases that held promise for a renaissance. All in all, the buildings were serviceable. New paint, signs, windows, and decorative touches distracted from the appearance of aging. The combination of office buildings, retail and small service shops showed signs of having been a real neighborhood.

Dizzy was getting used to working solo, but she didn't really like it. Her customary partner was testifying in a long drawn out case. This was his second week of unavailability.

She approached the crime scene and parked behind two other official vehicles, right next to an ambulance. First responders and police officials were scurrying about, taping off the area, taking pictures, inspecting equipment and labeling items they had placed in plastic bags. She passed through the gate and looked around the site. It was dusty and flat—a desolate valley surrounded by buildings rather than mountains. Unless there had been another injury, the ambulance was there to rush the victim to the morgue where the ME (Medical Examiner) would analyze the unspoiled body.

"Over here, Gillespie," the medical examiner called.

She reluctantly approached Dr. McCann, trying to look nonchalant. She hated the sight of corpses or copious bloodshed. She was troubled only slightly that her colleagues might recognize her reticence.

"Oh, over here, Detective Gillespie," the Medical Examiner repeated. The twinkle in McCann's eye showed that he was aware of her squeamishness.

Gillespie replied, "I'll be right over, Doctor." Under her breath she muttered, "You little imp." The forensic expert bore an uncanny resemblance to a leprechaun—small, sprightly, and sporting an outsized and very red drinker's nose. At times like these, he resembled a leprechaun more likely to appear as a villain in a horror movie than as a mascot on a box of Lucky Charms.

She glanced quickly but intently at the body. She created mental snapshots from different angles, including several close-ups. She methodically accomplished the task as quickly as she could. Later, she would rely on the expertise of specialists. As she averted her gaze from the body, she found herself eye to eye with McCann. If it was possible for eyes to smirk, McCann's were leering in the windows to his soul.

Gillespie took notes as the ME outlined his theory of what had happened. The victim had been shot twice from considerable distance just after the crew's 10:00 morning break. "Best guess is some sort of nut sniper. We can't figure why he didn't stick around to pick off more victims. No weapon or shells were discovered. So far the Crime Scene unit isn't even sure where the shots were fired from."

Dizzy departed from the corpse viewing and ME encounter and ran into a state police detective she knew from previous cases. He was a six foot four inch tall crew-cut trooper, neat as a pin. He had always been gracious with her. "Good to see you, Dizzy."

"Likewise, Lt. Conroy. Do we have anybody from the District Attorney's office working with us?"

He raised an eyebrow and pulled a cell phone out of what had to be too many holsters—even for a statie. He held up a finger to pause the conversation as he answered the call. "Yes, sir. Uh-huh. Her name is Detective Dahlia Gillespie. She's great to work with. I'll tell her."

He disconnected and turned to her and said, "His name is Latrobe. He'll be working on the case with you, but he couldn't change the docket on a case he's prosecuting today."

"That seems to be going around," Dizzy said.

He hadn't told the ADA that everybody called her Dizzy. Dahlia couldn't remember a time when she hadn't been called Dizzy. Derived from the famous jazz be-bop trumpeter who had the same surname, it was easier and friendlier than Dahlia. Her lazy eye, which meandered unpredictably—not unlike Peter Falk Columbo's glass eye—reinforced the name. Unlike Columbo, Dizzy was anything but rumpled: she was the department fashion plate. Whether in formal or casual attire, she always looked current, neat, and stylish.

Dizzy queried the patrolmen about their observations and interviews with witnesses and co-workers before she returned to the station. But they had nothing to add. Because of the noise and general tumult around the site, no one had actually seen the shooting.

At her office, she searched the files for a sniper or serial killer with a similar M.O. She hadn't yet received the detailed autopsy or the rest of the forensic reports, but she didn't expect many surprises. She would learn more about the victim and his situation soon. In the meantime, she searched photographs and the NCIC database online, talked to a couple of criminologists whose expertise concerned random murderers and snipers. By the end of the day, with no solid ties to a serial killer or the typical serial modus operandi, she returned to investigating the angle of a personal murder and the usual suspect.

The victim was married to Marilyn Parker. His full name was John Parker. Witness interviews had pieced together a profile of the victim. Since childhood, John had been known as "Jack" which had become "Jack Hammer" when he was working for public works. In fact, he had used the jackhammer quite a bit when he started out. Apparently as the years passed, his youthful washboard abs turned to a belly shake, rattle, and roll, and he gradually managed to spend more time expending less energy.

His reputation as one of the least active workers did nothing to tarnish his popularity. He had a keen sense of humor, and he created a new role for himself at the work site. He became the unofficial social director/morale officer—arranging gifts, playing practical jokes, placating disgruntled laborers, and getting the donuts.

Dizzy scheduled a visit with Mrs. Marilyn Parker. As she pulled up to the house, cars began to leave. The door was open as Ms. Parker politely ushered out a number of well-wishers and neighbors.

Now a widow, Mrs. Parker greeted her in a navy blue dress.

Dizzy showed her badge and asked, "Detective Dahlia Gillespie, ma'am. I'm sorry for your loss. How are you holding up?"

"People have been very kind, but it's wearing me down. I finally asked them politely to leave. They probably don't want to be here anyway. They're just trying to cheer up a sad woman."

Dizzy hesitated at the transom. "Would you be able to answer some questions?"

"Come in," Mrs. Parker said and showed the detective to a seat. "Coffee?" she asked. Her dark features were somehow appropriately somber.

"Yes, please. That's very kind." As Mrs. Parker went to the kitchen, Dizzy looked around the living room. It seemed homey enough, very lived in. Maybe too lived in. Although arranged to hide blemishes and scratches, the furniture was old and in need of some refreshing. Fabrics and carpets were worn and faded. On this occasion, her hostess looked a little faded herself. There were several photographs of Jack and a few of Jack and Marilyn together. The photos of Jack showed the almost inevitable belly growth of aging. He went from average to paunchy to pot-bellied—of the Dutch oven variety. No pictures of children, places, or friends or relatives. No vacation photographs. When her hostess returned with coffee, Dizzy began, "1 know this is a difficult time for you, Ms.

Parker. But I have to ask, was there anything different about your husband before he went to work the other morning or in the last few days?"

Mrs. Parker sat silently and stared off into the distance.

"Was he acting any differently the last few days?"

Mrs. Parker seemed to regain her focus, "No. Not that I can think of."

Dizzy paused for a beat, "Did he say anything to indicate that he might be in danger or did he mention any worries?"

Mrs. Parker slowly shook her head from side to side. A tear trickled down her cheek.

"Mrs. Parker, we'd really like to find who killed Jack and you knew your husband better than anyone else. Was there anyone you can think of who would want Jack—would want to hurt him?"

She continued to move her head in denial.

"Was Jack ever involved in politics...or with anyone you would consider dangerous?"

"No. He wasn't interested in any of that stuff."

Dizzy got the widow to discuss the marriage. It had been twenty years, up and down, but overall a good marriage. The couple had endured crises, overcome health issues, and celebrated good times. Then Dizzy asked, "Was he ever involved with another ....? Was Jack always faithful?"

"He was faithful. He was loyal." Marilyn Parker wept. Her tears streamed uncontrollably. Through sobs and whimpers, occasionally interspersed with trancelike silences, Marilyn expressed her grief—and her profound disbelief. "Jack was loved and so happy. No one who knew him would ever want to harm him. He was the nicest guy you'd ever want to meet."

"Is there a friend or someone from work who might be able to give me any information about Jack—outside of home?"

Mrs. Parker rose from her chair, "Not off hand, but you might check with Artie at work—Artie Rollins."

The neighbors intimated to Dizzy that Marilyn Parker didn't always treat her husband well. One neighbor even referred to Mrs. Parker as "HammerJack" because that's what she used to do. She would pick on

Jack endlessly. No one could recall her ever saying a kind word to or about her husband.

"I used to wonder about two things," said the man across the street. "First, was she hammering someone else? Second, when would she put the hammer on Jack?

Before Dizzy could begin along the well-worn path of suspecting the spouse, she spent some time interviewing other neighbors. Those who were closest to the Parkers thought that the comments were just Marilyn's manner. Some happy couples just sparred all the time.

Before she left the area, Dizzy checked in at the local church and a diner. Although there were signs that Mrs. Parker wasn't entirely satisfied with their finances, the consensus was that there was deep affection between husband and wife. Recalling the widow's tears, Dizzy agreed.

Artie's Take

Dizzy wanted to know more about Jack Parker. She decided to take the widow's recommendation. She called the construction company to arrange an interview with Artie Rollins. Learning that he was taking bereavement leave, she called and arranged to visit him at his home.

Unlike Jack, Artie definitely had a family. Toys and other wreckage adorned his home. Photographs of kids at various ages covered the walls. The hall was lined with photos of Artie with his plump but pleasant-looking wife.

Artie was a big guy in an entirely different way than Jack. He was raw-boned, tan and had the look of an athlete past his prime but still fit. Dizzy told him her purpose and Artie suggested a meeting in a coffee shop around the corner to avoid interruptions. His kids proved his point as their yelling in the background reached new crescendos. Artie said goodbye to his wife and he and Dizzy walked to the coffee shop.

They got coffees and sat in a corner with padded seats. Artie started the conversation. "I would like to help in any way I can. I'm totally devastated by what happened. I think I'm in shock." Dizzy waited. "I'm just now realizing how important Jack was to me. A great guy."

Dizzy asked, "Did Jack genuinely get along with everybody at the site?"

"Oh, absolutely. We all get along in general, but Jack was really well-liked."

Dizzy waited to allow Artie to gather his thoughts and elaborate.

Artie said, "You know, I've been thinking about him and why I miss him so much. He was thoughtful and kind. But almost as important, he was a great audience. He gave you his full attention. He laughed a lot and he was really enthusiastic about it. His laugh was infectious. It could sometimes have a ripple effect.

"So I suppose you can't think of any enemies."

Artie thought the question over. "No. None that I know of."

"How about his relationship with his wife?"

"Jack wasn't afraid to admit that he loved her very much."

Dizzy said, "Do I detect a 'but'?"

"No. Not really. I visited his wife—I mean widow—yesterday. I was sort of surprised at how much she was grieving."

"Surprised?"

"Well, those of us who had met Marilyn had some difficulty understanding why he loved her so much."

"Go on."

"She just didn't treat him well. She was kind of a harpy."

"About?"

"Probably money. She thought that Jack didn't bring home enough."

"How do you know that?"

Artie said, "Jack and I went out about a half dozen times a year to a local pub. When weather shortened the work day—you know, like sudden storms or the day before Thanksgiving and other occasions, we would end up together. We'd go out for a beer."

Dizzy prodded Artie for specifics.

Artie sighed, "I think that he and Marilyn really loved each other." He paused. "You know, from time to time he worried about money. He didn't make enough money to satisfy what he thought would make his wife happy. He started going to casinos to try to make additional cash."

Dizzy wondered, "How much did he think would have been enough?"

"I don't think that he really knew. He talked about getting Marilyn an engagement ring. A real engagement ring. When they got engaged, he was broke. As a joke, he gave her the paper ring from a cigar. He promised her a real one. Something symbolic."

Dizzy waited.

"He had me concerned. I've had other friends chase the jackpot and get themselves in trouble. For a moment I wondered whether his—the shooting—might have something to do with gambling."

"So you don't think that anymore. Why?"

Artie rubbed his chin, "Doesn't make sense. People don't shoot people who owe them money. There were no signs of threats or anything like that. And he said he was real close to getting a first class ring."

"What kind of gambling did he do? Do you know?"

Artie rubbed his face and thought. "I would overhear him talking about odds, big winners after some ball games, etc. He was interested. Certainly beyond the average sports fan. And I know he played the lottery."

"Don't most of the guys play the lottery, bet on sports?"

Artie said, "It just seemed to mean more to Jack."

"Did he have a bookie? Did he owe anybody money?"

"Not that I know of."

"Last question, Artie. If you were me, where would you look?"

Artie shook his head slowly, "I have no idea."

Dizzy said, "Thank you for your help. If you think of anything else, here's my card. Please call me."

Artie's voice shook. "You know I really think I got to know Marilyn a little bit. I felt bad about her being so alone."

"And?"

"She was so lost I offered to help her in any way I could. Jack never meant to leave her in this situation. I told her I could drive her to some appointments if we could arrange them for my day off on Thursdays."

"Artie, you're a good guy. Jack had a good friend in you."

"Yeah, but I didn't know it until now."

Dizzy emailed Assistant District Attorney Latrobe and filled him in on her progress—such as it was.

The ADA

The ground bounced up and down before Rob Latrobe. Drops of sweat hung over his eye, flying off every few strides. The sound of his breathing was uneven, raspy, but somehow comforting. For most of his jog, he imagined he was trail running as he used to. In his mind's eye, he was dodging boulders, roots, puddles, and mud. As he rounded the corner and slowed, he watched two shapely young women pass, their ponytails swinging like synchronized pendulums. This flora and fauna might indeed be better than those on the trail.

As always, he walked the last small stretch and arrived at home. He picked up the day's newspaper, went out to the porch to read and cool down. Steam rose from his body as he reclined on a patio chaise. As he found the sports page, he heard his wife's voice.

"How about a caffeine fix, Rob?" Kim leaned provocatively in the doorway. Well, maybe it wasn't meant to be provocative, but it certainly stimulated him. He looked at her and growled loudly and lasciviously. He wondered, not for the first time, how he, Rob Latrobe, had been so lucky.

"Down, young fella."

Rob Groucho-Marxed his eyebrows. "Is coffee all that's on the menu?"

"You can make yourself some cereal or a bagel."

"That's not what I had in mind."

"What mind?"

"Kim...."

"No ticky, no shirty. No time, no nooky." She leaned over, handed him his oversized mug, and kissed him quickly. "Tonight," she promised. Grabbing her keys and throwing her wrap over her shoulders, Kim rushed out the door.

Rob's growl became a whimper. He sipped his coffee, and went back to the sports page.

Forty minutes later, Rob Latrobe was knotting his tie, thinking how improbable it was that he and Kim had found each other. He still sometimes found it embarrassing. Well, not so much embarrassing as it was awkward to explain to people who didn't know them well. Others might not see beyond their age difference.

Kim was twelve years older than he was. At 5'5", she was a half foot shorter than Rob. People who met her found her pleasant and attractive. She could be a prototype for her Korean heritage. She was good-looking— dark eyes and hair, smooth skin and a winning smile. Her full lips and fuller breasts captivated men's attention. She worked in a small real estate office. While Rob's work as an assistant district attorney often left him exhausted at night, Kim's work energized her. She was fascinated by myriad disciplines—politics, television, mysteries, even her PC. At least once a week she stayed out with her coworkers for dinner and drinks. If Rob was lucky, it would be one of the several nights that he worked late. If not, he'd most likely be parked in front of the TV doing the Male Mambo with the remote, screaming at the Boston sports teams.

But bed time was their time. They cuddled. They hugged. They giggled. They talked. They made love. They slept. It was different each night, but it was intimate. They comforted each other.

Out of Site

It was a gray day, the kind of discouraging gray some thought only possible in New England, when Dizzy decided to visit the crime scene again. As she arrived at the end of the work day, a few remaining workers were preparing to depart for the night.

It was the scene of a crime, but no longer a crime scene. It was unencumbered by all the forensic professionals and evidence arrangers; the yellow tape was gone. Gillespie strolled around the area, and noticed that the pit where the victim had died was also gone—paved over in the wake of the continuing civil works project.

She tried to imagine the sights and sounds on the day of the shooting. The original pit site was cluttered with work in progress: trucks, backhoes, locked tool boxes, Porta-Potties and other paraphernalia. The area was flat and dry, punctuated here and there by scattered diggings. The smell of oil, asphalt and dirt invaded her nostrils.

She looked around at commercial buildings that surrounded the busy intersection where the work and its labor force had materialized. She watched trucks come and go; listened to the rumble of tires and the warning beep of backup lights. Horns blew as traffic was snarled and drivers grew tense.

The neighbors must hate the site. It interrupted their routines and their lives for months The nearby merchants and their workers had definitely been inconvenienced. Revenue had evaporated, customers had disappeared, and the project appeared to be no closer to its conclusion.

Taking into account New England winter weather, the optimistic end date was twelve to eighteen months away.

Dizzy created a vision of how it must have been on the day of the shooting. Co-workers had shed only limited light on the event. It had been typically busy. No one witnessed the shooting. No one heard it. No one saw it. No one even saw the victim go down. In fact, since the bullets had lodged in and possibly spun the body of the victim, the forensic team could only verify that the shot had originated from above.

Dizzy turned her attention to the neighbors. Three good-sized buildings stood near the construction site, one single story and next to it a three story office building with small retail shops on the street level. About a block away, a half-finished three story building looked as if planned to adjoin the other two buildings and expand the business environment. All of the upper stories offered unobstructed views of the crime scene. Good news for finding eyewitnesses, possible bad news for discovering where the shot might have originated.

Gillespie headed for the nearest building. The directory on the first floor listed several small businesses on the second and top floor. Those that had a view of the crime scene included an online magazine/blog, a dentist, a software developer, an IT/Computer Service Center, and a massage therapist.

Dizzy showed her badge and asked each office manager if she could look through their windows. All complied readily; murders didn't happen in their front yard every day. Curiosity about the shooting made her inquiries easier. Some tenants asked about the investigation. She asked them whether they had seen anything suspicious on that day and when they first knew a shooting had occurred.

Neither the interviews nor the views from the windows revealed anything helpful. The "blogger/journalist" Francis X. Bryan was intensely curious. Despite blond hair and startling blue eyes, he managed to be unappealing. He was sniffing around for some concealed corruption in the construction project. He looked intently at Dizzy and asked, "Did you know that the work site was vandalized a few weeks before the shooting?"

Dizzy said, "Tell me about it."

A look of self-satisfaction showed on the blogger's countenance—he knew something that the investigator didn't, "Someone did quite a job of wrecking things on the site."

"Who do you think did it?"

"The police assumed that it was kids," he said. "I thought it might be somebody whose business situation was devalued by the construction. Things have gone downhill for the businesses here since they started tearing things up. Almost couldn't blame someone for making them pay." Dizzy took his card as she had all the others, and decided she would look a little further into the activities of one Francis X. Bryan.

As she walked to the next building, she had the distinct feeling that she was being watched. A quick look around revealed no one suspicious. The second building was almost empty, most of the occupants having gone home. It was more than a block long with three entrances on each side. On the first floor a long narrow hall connected several offices of different sizes. Some had one door, others had as many as three. The entire second floor belonged to a law firm proclaimed in large ornate letters as *Reagan Walker and Esposito* with *Attorneys at Law* in smaller letters on a second line, and *Divorces, Torts, Personal Injury* still smaller on a third. She decided to leave the lawyers for a later date and walked over to the building under construction.

She took an exposed freight elevator to the second floor. She glanced back at the crime scene. This vantage point had been identified by the forensic team as a likely origination site despite the lack of tangible evidence. She had to agree that its isolation from foot traffic also made it a likely sniper's haven. As she gazed back at the construction site the feeling of being watched became stronger.

She walked toward her car, stopping at intervals to listen. Each time her own footsteps stopped, she distinctly heard others. She felt an odd combination of fear and detached humor. It was either a person following who could see when she stopped, or an echo or her imagination. Whatever it was, she was relieved to get into her car and leave.

Once home, Dizzy tried to relax by indulging in three of her favorite activities. She sipped an ice cold dry vodka martini. She listened to Arturo Sandoval, John Birks "Dizzy" Gillespie's greatest protégée. The original Dizzy had not only been an accomplished and innovative jazz musician, he was also a renowned mentor and teacher. Sandoval was a great trumpet player in his own right and, like his teacher, a proponent of Afro-Cuban jazz. She concentrated on the third activity lying open in her lap—the latest Dennis Lehane novel.

None of the three captured her attention.

A vague, elusive thought distracted her. Since her exploration of the vicinity of the shooting had uncovered nothing, she would seek more information about the victim. It didn't hold a lot of promise, but something skittered in her subconscious.

She sipped her martini and let her mind wander. Images of her past floated in her consciousness, blurring her examination of the facts of the murder. She imagined that she was floating above the worksite before, during and after the murder. It was a trick her father had taught her. "Try to become part of the background and observe. Pretend you're part of the scenery and use all your senses." Her ability to observe, understand, and relate to different types of people was one of her greatest assets. In school, nerds and jocks, insiders and outsiders, shallow and serious classmates all connected with her. In life, she could interact with black and white, males and females, conservatives and liberals, urbans and rurals.

Her ability to adapt or thrive in a variety of social situations was largely due to her natural tendency to like and trust people. They could sense her positive attitude and they reciprocated. Moreover, her father had taught her a great deal. He had been a salesperson, selling probably the most difficult products of all; he sold insurance and security services, and then high-end cars. "You have to be able to read people," he told his daughter at an early age. He taught her what to look for, to observe body language, facial expressions, changes in voice tone and more.

Occasionally he took his daughter on "field trips in search of truth." She looked forward to them because they would always end with ice cream. They would sit in a store or a car dealership and wager a quarter as to whether the customer would buy, whether the salesman was going to give up. Over time, Dizzy got it, and she began to win her share of quarters.

Dizzy had three older brothers and they taught her another life lesson. Not only did they protect her, they befriended her. Right from the start, she hung with the guys. Her ability to be one of the guys helped her later, especially when she joined the police force. She wasn't surprised by how men acted in locker rooms. She didn't have to consider whether she should laugh at an off-color joke. She laughed only if it was funny.

Now she was searching for motives for the murder. What if it wasn't personal? Maybe Jack Parker was a symbol. The noise, the blockades, the machinery and dust—these were more than inconveniences to the businesses around the construction site. The blogger had claimed that businesses in the area had slowed to an unreliable drizzle. It hurt the retailers most of all; the stores suffered precipitous decreases in foot traffic. Starting as an inconvenience, the construction had become an existential problem. On the day of and the day after the shooting, one of the store owners told a canvassing patrolman that the bustle outside her display window was "obstruction, not construction." Even the sub and pizza shops, whose sales had spiked significantly as they served laborers, believed that the area might not survive extended construction.

All the accumulated animosity might be a significant factor in the murder. Dizzy wondered if Jack Parker had offended one of the neighbors. The victim might have had a run-in with a neighbor or co-worker.

Thinking about the motives and mindset of the assailant and factoring in the construction situation, Dizzy began to wonder what recourse the neighbors had. Who had protested, what actions had they attempted? That reminded her of the second floor law firm. She decided to return.

Maybe it was all a waste. Maybe Jack had literally been in the wrong place at the wrong time.

Anger Management

Every day for over two months on the way to work, I passed the construction site. No matter how early I left, it always made me late. And I always hated it. I loathed the way the workmen seemed to be on a constant break, doing nothing. I despised the way nothing ever got done. One day a barrier would be put up. A week later it would be removed. Two weeks later it would be back. Pits would be dug. Pits would be filled in. And always, always traffic would be tied up. For no reason. People would be late and angry and frustrated. But nobody would do anything. Nobody ever did anything.

Julie Harvey waited. She had been waiting for The Patient to reveal specific issues. The therapy had been progressing deliberately up to this point. Almost too deliberately for Julie. She knew that there was often a warm-up process in psychotherapy. Time to develop trust. But in this case she wasn't even sure what the problem was, much less a solution. The Patient had come voluntarily, keeping problems as well as these sessions well-hidden from others—entirely secret. A romantic relationship had deteriorated, a job had gone bad, and drinking was problematic and occasionally showed signs of getting worse. The Patient could discuss and enumerate these circumstances—the kind that weigh on most people— but there had never been any overt expression of emotion. Almost like recitation. No acts of the kind that a person would only want to confide to a "shrink". No acts of almost any kind, The Patient seemed to just go along. Appearing to others as happy, or at least content. There was most likely a core of unhappiness so ingrained that The Patient finally made the positive move to seek psychological help. So far, that initiative hadn't proven successful. Now, after six sessions, a questionable or abnormal action finally started to become part of the conversation. Steadily and calmly.

One night I did something. As happened on too many nights, I was lying in bed recounting the things in my life that aggravated me. Each slight (and I may have imagined some) and most of the world's injustices intensified my anger, like lighter fluid dripping on an inflammable compound. I recalled so many things...

The Patient paused, seemed about to lose the thread. Julie prompted, "What kinds of things?"

Oh, so many—the least capable people advancing while the most inhuman and unethical people promoted them; newspapers and social media gossip with no proof damaging people's reputations; corporate executives getting paid way too much and getting away with too much. At the same time, the people who really do the work get paid way too little. It's unfair that the average person has so little to say, is so insignificant. The world is being run by corrupt and self-important politicians, ruthless gangsters, talentless celebrities, and wealthy, shallow business people.

Again Julie encouraged The Patient, "Specifically?"

Specifically, mortgage companies, landlords, unions, bureaucrats, the IRS, banks, and other callous and careless types.... like featherbedding construction workers.... Then my seething ignited. I exploded. I surged out of bed and frantically dressed. I tore through the garage and found what I was looking for. I threw on a jacket to insulate me from the night chill. My mind was racing and my heart was pulsating, my head felt like a coked-out drummer's sizzle cymbal. Still I managed to drive slowly. As if in a dream, my car seemed to drive itself, floating toward its destination.

I parked around a corner a couple of hundred yards away and out of sight of the site. It had agitated me and now it drew me like a magnet. I got out and walked slowly, dragging a heavy sledge hammer upside down so that the casual observer might take it for a cane or a crutch. The weight of the lead head forced me to limp, reinforcing my charade of a walking handicap.

When I looked back a few days later, I could recall the sensation of my three-legged walk, but not the specific details of what I had done. It was a blur of sound — breaking glass, snapping gear shifts and steering wheels, and general destruction. I remembered that when I returned the sledge hammer to my garage, I felt exhausted. Like I had finally done <u>something</u>.

When I drove past the site the following day, I half-expected to find the work site shut down, the obstacle in my daily life gone. Maybe I had smashed equipment, ruined the work site. Instead I found my problem compounded by additional police and other official cars investigating vandalism.

But I was in an entirely different frame of mind. For some reason, I could appreciate the irony. The delay no longer bothered me.

"What did you do after that?" asked Julie.

Sometimes it helped me tolerate some of the things that upset me, I began to think that I had actually <u>done</u> <u>something</u>; I wielded my "Hammer of Justice".

"Did you accomplish what you wanted?"

The Patient thought it over. *Within a few weeks the site from Hell went right back to delay upon delay. I guess it wasn't enough.*

The fifty minute hour was ending. Julie said, "Well, I think we're making progress. Before we meet the next time, I think it would be really beneficial for you to think about what you've told me today. How did your action ultimately affect you? How did it affect others? How do you assess it now that you've had some time to examine it?"

After The Patient left, Julie Harvey wrote some notes, recorded others from her half day of consecutive therapy sessions. She packed up her notes and files, locked them in the cabinets, and straightened out her desk. She locked her office and walked upstairs to her living quarters. Decades had slithered by since she had moved her practice into her home. She utilized a separate well-marked office entrance on the ground floor. It had worked out well and she couldn't remember why she had hesitated.

Her office in Boston had burdened her with a stressful commute. Her patients had to endure the lack of parking that cursed the city. But she stayed, immobilized by inertia—like a number of her patients. Two weeks after her husband passed away, she decided to move. She created the office for visits with a small waiting room insulated from the rest of the house. She lined a clear and inviting path with plants and flowering shrubs from the driveway around the side of the house to the office. Her shingle was midway between the driveway and her office door out of view from the street. From the very first day, she pledged to herself that her home and her office would be absolutely separate—as would her personal and professional life. With the exception of occasional snacks or beverages, nothing traveled from one region to the other.

The first activity she undertook after her last appointment was always the same—she took her dog for a walk. Siggy was her companion and at times her silent "advisor". The very adulterated border collie had been with her for about nine years. Playful as a pup, she was still a little frisky. Most important, she was a good listener, sort of a shrink's shrink. Julie would express her questions and speculations to her pet with some frequency. Siggy never ventured an opinion; she was the perfect sounding board.

They were at the lighthouse park, one of her favorite destinations (and Siggy's). On this occasion, Julie couldn't voice what was really bothering her. Instead she threw a stick for the canine to retrieve over and over. The psychologist couldn't convert her feelings into thoughts, never mind words. Her last Patient had left her with a feeling of foreboding. She knew that The Patient was hiding the truth, but that was expected in therapy. The process would eventually bring out the truth. It might be disastrous, but she felt the need to uncover the truth quickly. Whatever was roiling under the surface could grow and erupt, if it hadn't already.

She was aware that her ability to help others sort out their feelings and to work through their issues was a gift. She was really good at it. She sometimes appreciated that there was incongruity in all of this. She herself wasn't always happy. She was haunted by inner dark insecurities. Despite great success socially and professionally, something always gnawed at her, denying contentment or satisfaction. She compensated by indulging her sweet tooth, rendering her struggle with weight gain unsuccessful. Maybe that was why Siggy was so important. No judgment, just love.

The Patient sat and steamed in the car, watching the workers stroll around, oblivious to the problems they were creating in the lives of the people who paid them—the average taxpayer. Hadn't they learned their lesson? The Patient drove past the site and pulled left into a parking lot of a new and incomplete office building. The Patient shut off the ignition and exhaled deeply. This was going to be a new kind of justice, much more serious than the impulses The Patient had followed up to now. The Patient extracted a rifle case from the car as coolly as possible. The Patient got out, climbed the makeshift stairs, and found an opening overlooking the work site and removed a rifle from the case. The Patient carefully assembled the contents slowly to avoid attracting attention. The activity would appear normal and unthreatening to an observer.

The Patient squinted over the rifle sight, down into a hole and saw a large, sweaty man casually leaning against the far side wall of the pit, poring over what appeared to be a box of donuts. As a lanky co-worker walked away from the pit, The Patient fired. Nothing happened. The shot had MISSED. Even without a suppressor, the shots couldn't be heard over the traffic. The Patient fired again and again. Suddenly, in a weird pantomime, the fat man grabbed his stomach. As a second bullet struck, he jerked and disappeared. The Patient picked up the spent shells, wiped off the gun, put it back in the case, and left the area.

Peace Time

Before dawn, they got up to go hiking. To prepare for an early departure, they had stayed at Sheryl's place. Keith was on the futon; Sheryl in her bed. They groggily packed Sheryl's black SUV and took off for the mountains of New Hampshire. The ride was mostly silent. They were tired and after spending the previous evening together, there wasn't much to say.

America is mostly flat terrain. On the edges, the vast plains are bracketed by mountain ranges. Sort of similar to the graphic symbol for lodging—a flat line with one mountain range acting as a headboard and the other as a footrest. The west side features the Sierras and Rockies—spectacular, jagged, towering and seemingly infinite. Geologically, the mountains are young, still rising, still dynamic. On the east coast the Appalachian Mountains are smooth and eroded—older topography. The inhabitants in both places often reflect these factors.

The White Mountains occupy the New England portion of the Appalachian Trail and are a favorite of hikers. More navigable than the Rockies and defended from humans only by bears and weather, they offer serene beauty for relatively little effort.

Keith and Sheryl arrived at the trailhead and dressed for the hike on Franconia Ridge. Drizzle and mist enhanced the intrigue and challenge of a mountain hike. As they cinched up their backpacks in anticipation of a six hour trek, Sheryl reached into Keith's backpack.

"What are you up to?" he asked.

"I just wanted some of your world famous, double-barreled, gold-plated super-duper mega gorp."

"Well, it isn't in the back pack. It's in the side pocket...here."

He pulled out a bag and handed it to her. Sheryl poured out the contents into her hand. She ate small mouthfuls of a mixture of chocolate bits, M&Ms, peanuts, nuts, pumpkin seeds, and other snacking goodies. She rolled her eyes blissfully skyward and hummed, then continued on the trail, chewing.

They walked in silence for the first hour, drinking in the cool peace of the sun-dappled trail. Their eyes consumed colors and vistas. A mountain stream alongside the trail gurgled and glistened in the bright light, the sounds almost overwhelming their other senses. Cascades bubbled, birds warbled, and wind rustled the tops of the trees—all interspersed with silences. At one point, Keith scrambled deep into the trees to "Use the men's room." He was gone a while and Sheryl thought she heard metallic sounds and digging.

When Keith caught up, they both paused and listened to the wind as it moved around them above and beyond their view. They heard the clamor of something more forceful than the wind. Climbing over a rise, they stopped and gazed up at an immense waterfall. Its center was an imposing, near-solid sheet of white water, surging down, foaming into a clear pool at the bottom. On either side of the central flume, the water was clear, zigzagging over rocks, boulders, and granite slabs in trickles, fountains, and miniature spouts.

Without speaking, they headed for a large round rock near the center of the base pool. They pulled off their boots and socks and eased into the frigid water up to their knees, and with simultaneous groans, slung off their packs and equipment and sat down on a couple of flat rocks. The icy waters chilled their bones for about a second, relieving the soreness of their soles.

They drank from their canteens, stretched out on the rocks, inhaled the fresh mist and basked in the sun and shade. Sheryl broke the long silence when she told Keith, "You know an experience like this makes you think twice about the benefits of romantic relationships."

Keith said, "I understand. Believe me. Everybody seems to lament the great relationship that couldn't last. Only people who have been divorced talk about escaping a bad relationship."

Sheryl said, "I can. I once dated a guy pretty seriously for a while. Ending that relationship was one of the best things that ever happened to me."

Keith looked surprised. She went on to tell him about the aborted, abusive relationship she had endured—without mentioning Dan's name.

"Who was he?" Keith looked at her intently.

"He was somebody you know. And I'm over it so I don't want to ID him, ok?"

Keith thought it over. "OK, but If he ever bothers you, let me know."

She muttered, "OK."

Keith said quietly, "I mean it." Sheryl had the disquieting feeling that he knew she was talking about Dan.

They listened to the wind, the birds, water bubbling for a while. "Why do we put up with the day-to-day city shit when there's all this?"

"Yeah, just the sounds alone. Birds instead of phones."

"No cars."

"No gas. No smoke. No fumes."

"No crowds. No rush!"

"No pressure."

"No bullshit."

They sighed in unison, nestled in total comfort on the unrelenting slabs.

Keith pronounced, "If you ever want to get away," then paused.

As if on cue, Sheryl joined in on old refrain, "This is the place."

Firm Law

The key to unlocking the mystery of the construction worker's death was that there didn't seem to be any reason for anyone to want Jack Parker dead. Try as she might, Dizzy couldn't establish a motive. She had uncovered no illegal activity, no illicit romance, no profit motive—no revenge factor. Often the spouse was the most likely suspect, but not in this case. Not only did she seem genuinely sad, but all evidence pointed to a stable marriage and there was no indication of the kind of passion—e.g., jealousy or hatred that was requisite for a spousal homicide. Marilyn Parker had neither the opportunity nor the will to murder Jack. No, she was no murderer.

Then who did it? Lack of a suspect known to the victim led Dizzy in the direction of a sociopath or serial killer. But why hadn't he killed again? No drive-by public shootings occurred over the next several weeks. Sociopaths almost always stuck to their MO. Dizzy even monitored the rest of the country through the FBI database to find a similar case.

Nothing.

She checked in with ADA Latrobe frequently—a couple of phone calls, several emails exchanged. They were in sync but they hadn't met. He had been following up on forensics and checking traffic monitors and adjacent security cameras while at the same time he delved deeper into backgrounds of any acquaintances, including Artie Rollins. Nothing turned up. Dizzy was responsible for the legwork and they agreed to meet as soon as either one made any progress.

Dizzy called Walker, Reagan and Esposito; she explained that she was looking for more information about the community where the crime had occurred. The receptionist connected her to one of the names on the door. The partner agreed to gather as many of the attorneys and staff as possible for 11:00 the following morning.

Dizzy arrived early. She was greeted by a smartly attired receptionist and an offer of coffee. In a few minutes the coffee's aroma mingled with that of freshly cut flowers on the receptionist's desk. She was thankful that she had worn her gray tailored suit; it helped her fit in. People milled about—mostly males in suits and statuesque women. A couple of male attorneys passed by, jacketless and sporting open collar shirts. Ten minutes passed and the receptionist returned and led Dizzy down a hall into a brightly lit room. Surrounded by twelve comfortable-looking swivel chairs, a substantial modern conference table occupied the room. One wall was covered by a gargantuan video screen. On the other side of the table a credenza offered an array of pastries, coffee and other beverages. A wall of glass overlooked the site of the crime.

As Dizzy sat, the half dozen attorneys seated around the table ceased talking to each other and turned toward her. Dizzy introduced herself and passed out her business cards. In rote response, the attorneys returned the favor.

Dizzy opened, "I'm here to gather information that might help us with the investigation of the murder that occurred a few days ago. I'd be interested in your thoughts, both as lawyers in the community and as next door neighbors to the crime scene."

The attorneys shifted in their seats, glanced around. One of the younger male attorneys got up from his seat and poured a cup of coffee. The detective asked, "Did any of you see anything unusual or suspicious on the day of the shooting?" They looked at each other.

"I don't expect an eyewitness account, but your familiarity with the area and its routine could be helpful."

Again blank stares. Dizzy surveyed the faces in the room. "How about if you were me, where would you look?"

A lawyer with obvious gravitas piped up with, "At another law firm." The laughter eased the tension in the room. Another attorney replied to the first, "such as Monroe & Partners?"

"What kind of law do you practice?" Dizzy asked the first attorney. "And why Monroe & Partners?"

The well-manicured and dignified man in his fifties flashed a warm and genuine smile. "My name is Tom Reagan. I'm a partner in the firm. I practice family law, mostly divorces."

"And Monroe & Partners?"

"My colleagues are just yanking my chain because they know that Carl Monroe gets under my skin. He's the kind of lawyer who gives the profession a bad name."

Dizzy leaned forward, "How so?"

Jane Carpenter, the only female at the table, relieved the partner of what seemed to be a slightly uncomfortable spotlight, "he's only in it for money, doesn't care much about his clients' interests. He's worse than a P.I. attorney—which is what I am."

"P. I.?"

The attorney replied, "Personal Injury".

The digression relaxed the group. Reagan sat back. Dizzy became more direct. "So far no one I've interviewed who was in a position to witness the shooting has seen or heard anything. Why is that?"

"With the jack hammers and cement mixers, most of us have learned to tune out what was once an interesting view." Reagan pointed to the large window. The others nodded assent.

"Can you think of any reason for the shooting?" A brief discussion revealed that the construction had hurt or angered almost all of the business in the area as well as their customers, shoppers, and even those that depended on the affected businesses. "One of our neighbors on the block even asked us to pursue a class action suit against the town and the contractor," Jane added.

Dizzy reached into her blazer pocket and withdrew a business card. "Would that be Francis X. Bryan at *Frank's Blogkade?*" The attorneys nodded.

"What did you tell him?"

The others looked to Reagan who shrugged and said, "We explained that it wasn't really winnable. He wasn't pleased."

Again it was Jane who cut to the chase, "Off the record, we think that Bryan is a little off; there's something about him that makes us all a little uneasy." A couple of the others gestured agreement, another used her index finger to circle her ear, a very old symbol for a loose screw. Dizzy filed the characterization away mentally for future exploration and wrapped up, "Thanks for your time. If you think of anything, you have my card."

Cops Out

The Jury was convened. Otherwise the bar was relatively quiet and uncrowded. There was a sense of anticipation around the DJ table. In between topics, looking for something, the group's attention was drawn to the bar where a petite nice-looking black woman and a female uniformed cop sat down—Dizzy and a friend from work.

Dizzy scanned the room. She sensed a comfortable atmosphere, like a cop bar, but with a more diverse patronage. She saw no black faces in the bar. As she always did, she shrugged it off. However, she felt that there was something familiar about a couple of the groups hanging out together, but she couldn't figure out what it was. Was it a face? The clothing? The voices?

A voice interrupted her speculation, "May I get you ladies something?" It was the bartender. He was seasoned and self-assured. Dizzy guessed that he was the manager or owner. He was in fact both. Dizzy ordered a vodka martini, and feeling patriotic, she specified Tito's—an American-made vodka. Her friend ordered the same with a twist instead of Dizzy's olives. The bartender returned quickly with two perfect looking drinks. In a clipped and decidedly British accent, he asked, "Is this your first time here?" When they nodded, their host asked the question any smart retailer should, "How did you happen to come here? Friend's recommendation?"

Dizzy's friend said, "It was kind of an accident. We were walking and we just happened on it."

The bartender responded, "That's kind of how I found it. I just sort of wound up here. Liked it enough to come back. It reminded me of pubs in the Mother Country. Neighborhood place. Friendly, good honest food, inexpensive enough for people in the area to visit often." He pronounced the "t" in often. "My name is Michael Nielsen; I'm the proprietor."

Dizzy's natural curiosity kicked in. "What did you do before this?" She always liked discovering background information, whether from acquaintances or witnesses.

He sang, "I've been a pirate, a puppet, a poet, a pauper, a pawn and a king,"

For Dizzy such an indirect response usually meant that her interviewee was avoiding a direct answer. She suppressed her natural suspicion, but she was still interested in finding the truth. She gazed inquisitively at the barman.

He explained, "The ways I've made a living don't hang together very cohesively. At various times, and sometimes at the same time, I've been a locksmith, a real estate investor and agent, a sailor, a ballroom dancer, and for a time, a doctor."

Dizzy's companion asked with a big inviting smile, "Have you had any success?"

"Well, I've participated in international dancing competitions with a little success."

"I don't mean to be a wise guy, but how did you manage to squeeze in medicine? What were you, a tree surgeon?" Dizzy smiled at her companion's comment.

The barman himself smiled, "No, I got a degree in Grenada, but couldn't find a meaningful situation for my General Practitioner practice."

Dizzy and her friend looked at each other, almost exhausted by his life experience. The bar attendant sensed their desire to talk to each other and left them with some peanuts to munch on.

The other cop was even shorter than Dizzy and had black hair with matching large black eyes. Her name was Camellia Sanchez and she worked in forensics and intra-departmental communications. In their small station, some unusual hyphenated roles had to be filled. They had been working in the same station for several months and only said "hi". This was the first time they had socialized. Dizzy said, "You know I'm named after a flower too."

Camellia replied, "Is there a dizzy blossom somewhere?"

"No, my real name is Dahlia. Not as pretty as Camellia, so somehow I ended up as 'Dizzy'." Camellia smiled. Dizzy said, "I understand that this is your first job in police work. How are you finding it?"

"I last worked in an insurance office, so this should be much more interesting." She grabbed a peanut and said, "Dizzy, do you mind if I ask you a question?"

"As we detectives say, 'shoot'."

"Well, I've noticed that you seem comfortable in your skin…I mean as a female. Afloat in a sea of testosterone."

"And?"

"How did that come about? I don't think that the other women are as confident."

Dizzy thought and sipped. "You know I haven't really thought much about it. It wasn't conscious."

"Was there a point when you felt a change from being the "new" female to belonging?"

"I think it's about confidence. When you realize that you can do the job as well as others. Or at least you have some area where you excel."

Camellia raised her eyebrows quizzically.

Dizzy continued, "For me it was probably in self-defense class. I competed in judo when I was younger. It's one of the few places where being short can be an advantage."

Camellia prodded, "How?"

"It's all about leverage. The shorter person is more difficult to throw. The lower center of gravity can be a real plus. When I was studying judo and ju-jitsu, I gained a deep understanding of the principles. I threw the instructor a couple of times. After that I realized that between leverage and using your opponent's force to your own advantage, life could be a lot easier."

"Remind me not to mess with you."

"If you're good, I'll tell you about kuzushi and how to terminate aggressive assholes with extreme prejudice," Dizzy teased.

Camellia hesitated, then said, "You know when I first started on the job, I'm ashamed to admit that I heard rumors that you had advanced because you were kissing ass."

Dizzy's gaze almost penetrated her drink for one second. Then she softened, "Camellia, I would have guessed that a woman who advances gathers some rumors, but I would never do that. Under any circumstances."

Camellia nodded, "I already figured that out for myself."

Dizzy smiled, "You know the difference between ass kissing and brown nosing?"

Camellia said, "No I don't."

Dizzy whispered, "Depth perception."

On the other side of the room, the Devil's Jury waited quietly, some sipping their drinks, some studying the two newcomers until Dan broke the contemplation with, "They're both cops. I saw the one without a uniform investigating a crime." Heads turned slowly toward Dan.

"What crime?"

Dan responded, "That construction site shooting." Then in a loud whisper, "Did you ever notice how all the female cops on TV are really hot?"

There followed a discussion of sexy female cops from Mariska Hargitay to Alana De La Garza and Jennifer Lopez. Some had even seen Angie Dickinson in her prime in re-runs. Mostly they could only name the shows—Castle and Law and Order and the like. They dismissed the male counterparts as an aesthetically mixed bag.

Sheryl pointed out, "Isn't this a form of sexism?"

"Aren't you wound up tight as a cork?" said Ben.

The women nodded and the men clicked their glasses in a mock toast. "While we're on the subject of unrealistic TV cop shows, how about when the cops announce their presence to the suspect from a distance and then he runs away and they give chase?"

Dan noted, "My favorite is that every cop station has a genius geek who is accommodating and cooperative. I work with a lot of in-house IT people, but I have not found one yet that is really agreeable."

Dizzy and her friend departed, removing the impetus for the discussion and leaving the Jury trying to rate the attractiveness of the two female cops. Reality measured up well with fiction, and the unspoken consensus was that the two women were appealing.

Keith said, "I'm surprised that Danny Boy doesn't have some first-hand experience."

Sheryl said, "Meaning what?"

Keith went on, "when we were younger, Dan and I used to play as a duo."

Dan shouted, "Tell them what it was called."

"The Gruesome Twosome."

"What were our stage names?" Dan again.

Keith said reluctantly, "I was called Gruesome because I was the leader."

Dan, "You may think that was the reason …. What was my name?"

Keith waited a beat or maybe a full measure and said, "Handsome."

After a couple of catcalls, Keith continued, "We had a few gigs. Were busy for a time. Anyway, one Saturday night we got a last minute call from a fraternity. At first we turned it down because we each had plans."

Dan said, "But they offered us a lot of money. So we broke our plans, dropped everything and went to the fraternity party over at the university."

The story was almost becoming a verbal duet, and Keith came back with, "when we got there; there was another act playing and the boys at the frat house wouldn't let us in. We asked for the guy who had hired us and were told he was busy. Dan told them to get his ass in front of them. They tried to push us off, but Dan was having none of it."

Dan was obviously recalling the event and his eyes were almost glowing.

Keith said, "The guy showed up. He was really arrogant and admitted that he had in fact promised us the gig but had changed his mind. Dan flew into a rage and pounded the plaster wall inches from the kid's face with a karate chop and scared the Bejesus out of Mr. Arrogance. 'Get our pay or I'll break every window in the place.'"

Sheryl asked, "What happened?"

Dan said, "We got our money."

Everybody applauded and Dan raised and drained his Jack Daniel's.

Torn Asunder

Sheith was not an exclusive association. Sheryl and Keith were often joined by Keith's brother. Larry was close to the two of them and it was common for him to see them without his wife, especially when they wanted to see a "popcorn" movie. One such occasion proved to be pivotal in their lives.

On the giant cinema screen a small, agile Asian tore off his shirt, revealing a muscular body worthy of an Olympic gymnast. He struck the prototypical Kung Fu pose. He snarled at the horrific-looking green alien. In the darkened theater, Larry leaned over and whispered to Keith, "We've got to talk."

After watching the Kung Fu practitioner vanquish the alien (and its whole family) with a combination of martial arts, explosive weapons, and magic, Keith, Sheryl, and Larry went out into the night. "Did you see when he did that double back flip and kicked both the monster and his crony at the same time?" marveled Keith.

Sheryl responded, "Did you see his buns?"

"Did you catch the way that CyberLaser followed the Gretschel around the shield and creamed him?" Keith continued.

Sheryl responded, "Did you see his buns?"

"...and the way it gushed orange and black goo instead of blood? That was the wildest..." Keith stopped walking and talking and stared at Larry. Two strides later, Sheryl stopped and slowly turned to stare at Larry.

Larry returned the look. It was unlike Larry to be so quiet. The silence was palpable. As it grew among them, Larry's eyes misted over.

They sat on a park bench and he filled them in. "It was such a god-damned cliché. Everything appeared to be fine. Fine, but no longer fun. Carolyn was too quiet. Distant. I asked her what was wrong. More than once. She always said 'nothing'. Once she said she wasn't happy. Just once. She wouldn't tell me any more. Every time I asked her what was wrong, she said nothing. Then one night after the kids were in bed, she just turned and said, 'I want a divorce!'"

"Oh my God, Larry," said Sheryl. Keith just shook his head slowly.

After a long silence, Larry mustered a smile to relieve the tension. "It's really kind of awful. Losing her is bad enough. Divorcing her is worse."

Keith interrupted, "What do you mean? When did this happen?"

Larry looked his brother in the eye, then at Sheryl, "Almost three months ago."

Keith and Sheryl looked at each other in total disbelief; his concealment was almost as shocking as the breakup itself. How could he have kept it a secret?

Larry continued, "she promised that we'd always be good friends. You know, we were not going to get into any messy lawyer scenes."

As they rose and walked a little further, Keith and Sheryl each silently reviewed the past few months. They recalled Carolyn's absences, Larry's increased availability, Larry palling around with Dan, and his frequent insistence on being the last one to go home from the bar or anywhere else.

"Where does it stand now?"

"It didn't work out the way she said it would. Carolyn hired an attorney. We're separated. I got a place of my own."

Keith asked, "Are you divorced?"

"Not yet. It's like a slow death. My life has become the legendary hell of litigation run amok."

Larry explained how every detail of the divorce had become a source of bitter contention. Nothing was reasonable. Carolyn had only one purpose in life—to hurt Larry. Keith and Sheryl guessed that the venom had been injected by her attorney—Carl Monroe. "The divorce hijacked every part of my life."

In many ways it took over all their lives. Sheryl was concerned, hurt and angry, and Keith vacillated between seething and ballistic for a long time.

Piece Time

Carl Monroe rocked gently in his black high-back leather "Judge's Chair" and bridged his fingers on his ample stomach. He playfully completed a swivel as he surveyed his well-appointed mahogany office. He paused and swung back to look at his collection of chess sets. He had bought his first set after his first big case. That was the case that became the model for his considerable success. With divorce cases, you didn't measure success by winning or losing. More than any other kind of case, success was measured only in dollars. He had learned how to make serious money in divorce cases.

You let them grow. You delicately combined passive aggressive neglect with periodic agitation toward the spouse. You withheld support to your client when he or she was already enraged and then you colored the opposition red and waved that flag in your client's face at the first sign of conciliation.

After the first case that earned him more than $75,000, he visited the exclusive shop across from his office thinking he should buy something expensive to celebrate and commemorate. The shop specialized in estate collectibles. Until now, he had only glanced in the window. Solely on a whim, this time he entered the shop. Most of the merchandise was too old, too frilly, and too ornate, but, he realized with great satisfaction, no longer too expensive. Divorce attorneys were not well-loved, often held in little more esteem than the Black Plague by colleagues, opponents, and the public alike. To Carl, the money was well worth the enmity. After all, unlike most legal practices, divorce attorneys handled cases rather than clients, one and done and on to the next.

The ivory chess set in a far corner of a long, low glass case caught his eye. It was captivating. The quantity and accuracy of the details were astounding. He had to have it. What could better represent his work than chess? It was an ancient and respected game whose outcome depended on crafty strategy and rapier-like tactics.

Today after almost eight years, several bitter divorce cases, and well over six million dollars, he had an expansive and expensive collection. As he fondled a piece from each set, he found it difficult to remember some of the individual cases which had occasioned his acquisitions.

As was his custom, the last piece he picked up was his favorite. A black king. This one made of carved onyx, the most ornate piece in the game. He felt its smooth contours and thought dreamily how the king on the board was similar to him on a case. All the moves enhanced his position and the game couldn't go on without him.

Financial success wasn't all champagne and caviar—although it could be. He had very little time to enjoy his palace-like house. Nor could he make it a home with a wife and family. His own Machiavellian maneuvers made it difficult for him to trust others. He suffered from an unfounded but undeniable suspicion that others were only interested in his money. All the people in his life—his travel agent, his pool service, his tailor, and the bartender at his favorite bar—were paid relationships. He had a special regard for wait staff that he knew. He only frequented establishments where they would address him by name. He treated them well, was friendly and generous. However, he could be nasty and condescending to those who didn't know him—doormen, cab drivers and other service people.

He replaced the piece and exhaled. He placed some papers from his desk into his briefcase and snapped it shut. Removing his camel-hair coat from its hanger, he turned off the lights, and left his office.

Carl Monroe stepped out into a gray dusk. He took in his first breath of fresh air in several hours and marveled at the clarity of visibility as daylight waned. He headed toward his silver Lexus in its reserved space in the parking lot across the street.

In less than a half hour, he would be home. He could almost taste his dinner. He would take advantage of living on the North Shore, on the Atlantic. Fresh seafood. His personal chef would have fresh chilled lobster and clam chowder ready once he walked in the door.

Then he heard the urgent squeal of tires. He turned toward the sound and froze when he saw the SUV bearing down on him. It accelerated straight for him. He rushed for the sidewalk and the car swerved to follow him. The last thing Carl Monroe saw before the impact flipped him into the air was the determined smile on a driver's face he recognized. He could not recall from where; he could not understand why.

Hit-and-Run

As an Assistant District Attorney, Rob Latrobe pushed a lot of paper. There was more paper now than ever—in addition to tons of documents on hard drives. He spent his time plea bargaining, jousting for good cases, filing motions, chasing witnesses, collecting evidence, researching precedents and working with and occasionally second-guessing police.

Rob was knotting his tie, getting ready to leave for work when his phone rang. The call was from The Motor Vehicle Homicide Unit. The state had established the unit as a cooperative effort between local police, state police and designated Assistant District Attorneys. They were on call to investigate vehicular homicides. Rob had been a member of the unit, but had not been called upon to participate in a case—until now.

Rob drove directly over to the scene to investigate. Often there was a driver to be charged. Sometimes not. Typically, vehicular homicides involved alcohol or other intoxicants or extreme negligence. Rob's first case of vehicular homicide turned out to be a hit-and-run—the most difficult kind of vehicular homicide to resolve. This case turned out to be a real "who-done-it". The driver had taken the "run" part in earnest. He (or she) was nowhere to be found. No reliable witnesses.

In most urban cases like this one, there were witnesses who could at least identify the make, model, or color of the homicidal vehicle. In some cases, the witnesses even noted all or part of the license plate number. Those were the easy ones. Then there were cases outside the city or at off-hours in the city when there were no witnesses. In those instances, there was almost no chance that anyone would ever be caught.

Finally, there were those odd cases when someone would come forward and confess. Many did so. Most were not criminals. They were ordinary people who had made an error, had an accident. Often under the influence of drugs, liquor, outright misery, murky darkness or other distractions, their lives changed in an instant. In the bright sunlight of contemplation, the taking of another human life often proved too much to bear.

Once at the scene, Rob saw that the body was gone and only blood stains remained. The victim was a lawyer named Carl Monroe. The street was a well-populated side street in the city—not made for high speeds. The sky was gray but backlit and the pavement was dry. Three people witnessed the aftermath of the accident. One of the three thought she heard the victim scream "no" and thought he had tried to evade the vehicle. But she wasn't sure. It had happened too fast. They all saw the car leave the scene, wheels squealing. Remarkably, they all agreed on a description of the vehicle. It was a black SUV or other 4-wheel drive car.

Black SUVs were pretty common. Rob put out an alert to body shops and auto dealerships. He reported the description to the press, and hoped that the driver felt guilty enough to turn himself or herself in.

Investigating the scene revealed little out of the ordinary. He decided to view the body at the morgue.

When Rob entered the mortuary, he was approached by the medical examiner on duty, Dr. McCann. "Hi, Mr. Latrobe, I'm Dr. McCann. It's about time we met in person. I understand you're here for my report on the hit-and-run victim."

Rob shook the ME's hand. They had spoken on the phone and Rob had received copies of reports from him. "That's right. All I know is that his name is Carl Monroe. What else can you tell me.?"

"Well, there was no doubt about his C.O.D. He was hit square on. Hard. The car must have been going pretty fast."

Latrobe responded, "Witnesses didn't see or hear much before the thud of a car hitting the body. Then the car sped away—no hesitation. Does the body tell us anything?"

"Nope," McCann passed up the opportunity for one of his standard quips "contrary to popular belief dead bodies don't really talk." He pondered for a moment as Rob turned to leave. "I can tell you that the victim was a lawyer," he paused as if contemplating whether he should continue.

Rob waited. When no comment was forthcoming, Rob turned on his heel again.

The doctor stopped him with "the kind of lawyer most people are talking about when they say that they hate lawyers."

Rob sensed something under the surface, something intriguing, "how so?"

"Let's just say that he wasn't well-liked around the courthouse."

"Is that all?"

The doctor looked at his watch as though he had something else pressing, a hint that he wanted to end the discussion.

Rob pressed a little, "Is there anything else, Doctor?"

"You hear things. Some of the other attorneys and even his clients didn't like him… or trust him." He paused, "Not surprising. He was a divorce attorney. Very aggressive."

"Thanks, Doctor."

Rob left the office with a nagging feeling about the accident. Whatever he could deduce about the hit-and-run flowed from one inescapable circumstance—there was no apparent cause for the accident. The street was clear. The visibility was clear. What was not clear was why the accident happened. Unless it wasn't an accident…. Rob reminded himself that a hit-and-run was a homicide and might be the perfect method for pre-meditated murder. Maybe he had read too many murder mysteries, but approaching the death as an intentional homicide introduced new questions. Unless it was a random *act of God,* knowing more about the victim now became paramount.

The next day Rob tended to his other work. Much of it was tedious, and it occurred to him that the hit-and-run case could offer a break in his routine as well as a new opportunity and a new challenge.

It was surprising how quickly practicing law in an eastern suburb on the North Shore of Boston had become Rob's routine. He had lived in the area for less than two decades. Still it was quite a change from the first part of his life. He had grown up in Panguich, Utah, a town that still looked like the Wild West—because it was. It maintained wide open space with less than one person per square mile—comfortable but culturally restrictive.

Raised by a foster family, Rob had never known his birth parents. He was somewhat of a novelty being a gentile among his Mormon neighbors. Almost all of his neighbors and friends were members of the Church of Latter Day Saints. Rob did gain an appreciation of some of the mores of their faith. He was enthralled by their devotion to missions and he did identify with many of the "us against them" attitudes, as well as their dedication to community and family.

As an athlete, he had a chance to make friends and he was as happy as most teens—which is to say, not very. His grades were better than average, but he was no scholar. When he was in high school, he decided that his community was too homogeneous and determined to venture beyond its limits. He arranged to meet his only blood relatives outside the area. During the summer of his junior year in high school, he stayed with his aunt and uncle outside Boston. Researching colleges was the ostensible reason for his trip.

He had expected the East to be different, but the differences were more profound than he could have ever anticipated. He had known it would be faster-paced, noisier and more crowded than his small hometown. However, he wasn't prepared for other changes. There was an overwhelming variety—of everything—foods, places, directions, clothes, stores, and entertainments. Most of all, the people fascinated him—diverse colors, ethnicities, styles, and viewpoints. There were more houses of worship for more sects and religions than he ever could have imagined.

Of course, when he arrived at his relatives' home, he was at an age when liquor would have interested him more than religion. Surrounded by Mormons, liquor hadn't been in demand or in long supply. In Boston alone he discovered that a single liquor store offered more brands and types of spirits than he had seen in all of Utah.

As if these discoveries weren't dissonant enough, Rob was totally surprised by the area's age and history. New England had been central to the nation's founding, was immersed in history, tradition, and American culture. More than two centuries before whites came to Utah, the Boston area had been evolving as a colony and nation. Over four centuries, architecture developed, technology advanced, and urban culture blossomed. Unlike Utah, Boston was very European—revolution from England, evolution from Europe. Living on the North Shore of Massachusetts, Rob became enthralled with colonial history, witches, the Revolutionary War and other reminders of older times. He went to a community college on the North Shore, then finished at the University of Massachusetts, worked hard, graduated with honors, and went to Boston College Law. BC Law was well-respected and opened some doors at firms and in government. After a short stint at the law boutique of a fellow alum, Rob became an Assistant District Attorney for Essex County. ADA Latrobe had researched, negotiated, prepared briefs, advised, and tried criminal cases, mostly misdemeanors. Now he was directly involved in two major crime investigations.

Re-Group

The members of the Devil's Jury started to arrive at Bar None in the late afternoon. By 7:30, most had drinks in front of them. Short exchanges chronicled recent events, activities, news, and weather. Less than an hour later, laughter and drinks proliferated and conversation warmed up. As was their habit, the participants briefly ridiculed several celebrities for their drug addictions, marriages and divorces, or screw ups in social media or on the playing field. They called these pot shots at the rich and famous *Xquisitions*—one more reminder of the Inquisition. These "star shootings" went on until some specific subject distracted them.

Tonight's topic was determined when an older couple shuffled in, sat at the bar, and ordered drinks. Some in the group recognized them as regulars. Larry asked, "Who's the oldest person you know?"

Keith answered, "You are, sometimes."

"No seriously, how old is the oldest person you know well?"

People shouted out numbers, mostly in the 80's. Sheryl mentioned that she had a neighbor who was ninety three, and she knew that because he told her almost every time she saw her. "He goes for walks which I call 'limps' almost every day. I usually see him when I get home from work."

"Maybe that's not an accident; maybe he has a crush on you," ventured Keith (winking at his brother Larry).

"Well I can tell you that he looks better walking than you do on our hikes," Sheryl smiled. The group turned to Sheryl and like Roman citizens they each in turn dramatically gave her the thumbs down.

Sheryl shrunk back in mock fear, "Oh no, condemned by a Devil's Jury of my peers." No one could have foreseen what the sentence would be.

The night wore on and the group amassed a significant list of senior citizens that they knew. Ben said, "It must be tough, just kind of waiting to kick the can."

Larry said, "Yes, it must be. They can't kick the bucket down the road like younger people." Ben was the only one who didn't appreciate the way Larry had imitated Ben's maiming of clichés.

The discussion revolved around retirement, hearing difficulties, and memory loss.

Keith said, "Did you know that restaurants have turned to ROMEOs to replaced customers lost to unemployment and recession?"

Sheryl asked the question that could have been too obvious, "Romeos?"

Keith smiled, "Retired Old Men Eating Out." They chuckled as Keith explained that lunch and breakfast business seemed to be on the uptick in the area.

Dan thought that the conversation was getting a little dull—or at least serious, "You know there is an advantage to getting older…" They waited for what they knew would be a punch line.

"You can hide your own Easter eggs."

Keith took that as a cue and he slipped behind the bar as he often did to help clean up. The group dispersed.

Sheryl walked home from Bar None that night still smiling from the last remarks of the evening. She was enjoying the crisp autumn air and feeling pretty good. Maybe it was the drinks or the collegial interactions she had just enjoyed at Bar None. Whatever it was, Sheryl was ambling leisurely and contemplating her situation, now that Dan had been out of her romantic life for a while. Suddenly she became aware that she was being followed by a slow-moving vehicle. In a matter of seconds, she knew that the car wasn't just driving slowly; it was in fact following her. She looked around quickly and noticed a glow ahead. It was the work site where the murder she had read about had occurred. It was well-lit and conspicuously located. She thought if she could reach it, she'd be safe. She took out her cell phone. Rather than trying to put in her password, she pretended she was talking to someone. With her other hand she took out her flashlight—all without breaking stride.

The lighted destination was less than a hundred yards away when she became aware of someone walking behind her. She hadn't heard a car door, but she knew that's where her stalker had come from. Then she heard the creepiest voice she had ever heard. "Oh, Missy, want to party?" He was about ten feet behind her. Sheryl paused for one second. Then she wheeled and took three long, quick steps toward her would-be assailant. She feinted a kick to his groin. He reacted, looked down and instinctively brought his hands down to protect his crotch. She struck him in his windpipe with the flashlight. He staggered back, holding his throat. Then she kicked him square on his knee. He went down and she shined the beam at the occupants of the car and started screaming, "You're under arrest!"

The car sped off. She watched her erstwhile attacker writhe on the ground, and then she ran into the work site and called 911.

Several lights went on in the area and the police arrived ten minutes later. She rode in the police car the two blocks to her home. Once inside, she drew a bath. Lying in the warmth of the water, she thought that her recent self-defense course had paid off.

In a perverse way, she could thank Dan. She had been upset by her reaction to his treatment—the fear she felt when Dan was in a tirade. In much the same way that many people think of what they *should* have said after the argument is over, she chose an unusual way to fill the vacuum left by Dan. She had enrolled in a self-defense class. She was reminded of the cliché that "what doesn't kill you makes you stronger". Her new-found confidence and sense of accomplishment had definitely made her stronger—and happier. Her next step would be to buy a firearm. Learning how to shoot would be fun. And it could be useful.

The Ring

Marilyn Parker had been doing her best to live with her husband's death. She forced herself to manage all the obligations that came with being a widow—obtaining a death certificate and informing the IRS, organizations, credit cards, his union and the like. She had to pay debts and stop obligations. She had to apply for survivor benefits with social security. The small amount coming from Jack's life insurance policy would help.

She was feeling alone and cast adrift as she sat and looked around her living room. Children would have been a comfort and a possible source of support. Her only life had been her life with Jack. She would have to find a way to survive and then eventually a way to thrive.

The doorbell rang. She got up to answer it. It turned out to be a certified letter from a nearby bank. It wasn't a bank she used. She hoped it didn't concern some sort of debt or oversight. The letter told her that in compliance with state law and the bank's by-laws, as Jack Parker's widow, she was entitled to be present when his safe deposit box was opened and she would receive its contents. Safe deposit box? Marilyn had no idea that Jack had ever visited that bank. She couldn't imagine what he would keep in a safe deposit box. Why had he kept it a secret? Had he led some kind of double life?

The more she thought about it, the more anxious she became. She couldn't ignore it. She called the signatory of the letter, a Ms. Cleary, to set up an appointment to come to the bank. Not wanting to go alone, she called the one person who had been actively supportive—Artie Rollins. In the days and weeks following her husband's death, he had called every couple of days and asked how she was doing. He offered to help her if she needed it. He had helped her on two occasions—once to help her dispose of clothes and several other items and once to fix a broken end table which looked like it had been broken intentionally at some point.

Artie agreed and accompanied her to the bank. They satisfied an identification process and Ms. Cleary gave Marilyn a key and explained that it was hers for the remainder of the year paid for by Jack. Then she ushered them into the vault housing the safe deposit boxes. Ms. Cleary's used Marilyn's key as well as her own to unlock a small safe door. They removed a long storage box, and carried it into a quiet room with a Spartan desk and chair and waste basket. Ms. Cleary left them and told them to knock on the door when they were ready.

Artie and Marilyn stared at the box for a moment. Artie could sense Marilyn's trepidation. She was visibly shaking.

Artie tried humor. "Maybe it's a Maltese Falcon."

She shook her head.

"It could be the recipe for McDonald's Secret Sauce. You'll make a fortune."

She forced a smile to humor him.

"Maybe it's money that Bernie Madoff hid?"

That broke through. Marilyn caught the spirit and put the situation into perspective. "I certainly hope so. It's the least that Jack could have done."

"Even better, maybe it's the ring."

"Which ring?"

"You know, the Lord of the Rings ring."

Marilyn looked at Artie and opened the long metal lid. Inside were a document and a small felt box that looked like a ring box. She slowly opened the box. She gasped and stepped back. "It is the ring."

Artie stepped closer and peered in. And understood.

It was a beautiful and tasteful diamond ring. Marilyn took a step forward and picked up the ring. It was the ring she had always wanted. The ring. How had Jack managed it?

"This was the ring I always wanted; Jack could never afford it." She sobbed.

Marilyn put the ring on and turned her hand to catch the light—just like a new bride. Tears glistened on her cheek.

She unfolded the document. It was a life insurance policy on Jack for $100,000. It hadn't been dated and signed, but the date was recent, this year in fact. She thought that it would have been better if he had signed it. Much better.

It would have been even better if he had lived.

A Ghost of a Chance

Keith was a little quieter than usual the next time the group gathered at Bar None

Larry prodded his brother, "What's shakin', Bro?"

Keith said, "Nothing much." Larry looked at him and then they ordered "the usual" drinks.

Ben arrived late, looking weary if not sickly.

Keith said, "OMG, Ben. You look terrible. Like a ghost, or at least like you've seen one."

"I've had a lousy day. I got out of bed on the wrong foot," said Ben.

Larry said, "Speaking of ghosts, do you guys believe in them? Has anyone ever seen one?"

Sheryl said, "Only in movies. You know, Christmas Past, Hamlet, and Casper."

Dan said, "Have you noticed how ghosts have become gentler, more benevolent? They're usually in comedies. We don't take them seriously any more."

Sheryl said, "I have a favorite ghost." The group turned to her. "Patrick Swayze. He can haunt me anytime."

Keith said, "Has anyone ever seen a ghost? What about spirits?"

Dan said, "I drink them all the time" and downed his shot of Jack Daniel's in demonstration.

Larry said, "I think that most cultures believe in animal spirits. I've had some of my friends who hunt talk about the spirit of their prey. In an admiring way."

The general consensus of the group was that they didn't believe in ghosts—or much else that they couldn't see or touch. Ben said that he didn't believe in ghosts or an afterlife.

Sheryl looked at him with concern, "What do you think happens after you die?"

Ben replied, "To be or not to be that is the question."

"Unfortunately the question isn't 'to die or not to die," said Larry.

Keith and Sheryl stared at Ben in disbelief and commented in unison, "Did Ben get that Shakespeare quote right?"

Dan said, "You rot. You decay. You eventually turn to dust."

The group took sips and digested the discussion up to that point.

Dan said, "Sometimes I think the spirits of my parents and grandparents are around on St. Patty's Day."

Larry said, "Of course you do. You're literally filled with spirits then."

Ben said, "I don't believe in an afterlife or a god or reincarnation. Or ghosts. But I visit my parents in the cemetery from time to time to show them that I haven't forgotten them."

Keith said, "Ben, that makes no sense. It's a contradiction."

Ben shook his head slowly. "I know."

Most of the group agreed.

After a long minute of silence, Dan piped up with, "I believe in genies!" The group knew he was setting up the adjournment joke.

They raised their glasses in a salute to what was coming. Dan leaned back, "So this guy frees a genie from a brass lamp. He says to the guy, 'You have freed me from a thousand years imprisonment. I will grant you three wishes.' The guy rubs his hands in glee. But the genie tells him there's a catch."

Ben and Larry chimed in together, "There's always a catch."

Dan continued, "The genie explains, 'whatever wish I grant you, your wife will receive more of.' So the guy says I love golf, I want to be a scratch golfer. The genie grants the wish but warns the guy that his wife will be two under par, then says, 'what's your second wish?' The guy says I want to be a millionaire. Genie grants his wish but tells him that his wife will be a billionaire. 'What's your third and final wish?'"

Dan paused and finished, "The guy says 'I'd like a mild heart attack.'"

A week or two later Keith was cleaning the table after the group broke up. Dan remained seated after the others had gone. He was anxious; he seemed to be waiting for something—or someone. As Keith thought about it, he realized that Dan had been acting strangely for a while. He arrived late a couple of times and was distracted. He was strangely remote and when he related his stories and jokes, he wasn't genuinely involved. It was like he was playing a role. He was playing the role of Dan rather than being Dan. Dan nursed his last drink, waiting for a call or some event. Keith cleaned while Dan waited. Finally his cellphone rang, and Dan got up and left. Out of curiosity, Keith followed.

Dan walked deliberately, but not hurriedly. The sidewalk was moderately crowded with a steady flow of pedestrians. Keith kept rhythm and stayed behind in the crowd. He followed Dan for two and a half blocks. He had no idea where he was going or what to expect. Strangely, he was experiencing anxiety mixed with excitement and a feeling of adventure. He turned a corner and saw Dan standing, as if waiting for something or someone. As if on cue, an SUV glided alongside and stopped. Dan opened the passenger door and eased into the seat and leaned over and gave the driver a lingering kiss. When the driver turned forward, Keith saw that it was his former sister-in-law, his brother's ex-wife—Carolyn.

The Black King

Assuming that the driver of the death car knew the victim, Rob visited Carl Monroe's house. It was fairly impressive, large and beautifully and professionally landscaped. Only the giant koi floating in the small ornamental pond in the back were reminders of the recent demise of the owner.

The elegant décor had obviously been designed by a professional. More a showroom than a home. The walls featured giant modern art interspersed with degrees and awards that Monroe had received in his career. Rob didn't turn up anything that could lead to the identification of his killer.

Next he visited Carl Monroe's office. Since it was not a crime scene, Rob simply walked in and presented his credentials to a lone secretary. She was in her late forties and looked as though she had been thinner at one time. Now she was slowly cleaning out her possessions from the reception area, a small file room, and a coffee/kitchen area. She trudged back and forth, taking little or no notice of Rob. He reintroduced himself verbally by asking for a cup of coffee. "There's a Keurig in there. Help yourself."

"Thanks, Ms....?"

"Diliberto, Miss Carmen Diliberto, Mr. Latrobe," she finished his sentence.

"I'm sorry for your loss, Miss Diliberto."

She suspended her activities and turned to Rob, "It's really just a job."

"What can you tell me about Mr. Monroe?"

"Not much, he was very ambitious... and successful. He treated me ok..."

Rob picked up on her tone, "I sense a 'but'"

"No real 'but' but I realized after the accident that I didn't know Carl very well. I was here for six years, and other than some fits of anger over slow payments or jubilation over big fees, he never showed his true feelings. I didn't really know him." She looked around the room, "He was a bachelor. You could say confirmed. Once in a while he would take a date to an event he thought he should attend. But I don't think he really enjoyed it. He had no family or relationships that I'm aware of."

Rob said, "Can I look in his office?"

They entered Monroe's inner sanctum. Leather, wood, and brass. One plant—a Venus' flytrap—a note was attached "To a great human being—use it well—T.R." The carnivorous plant was obviously meant as a comment or a joke. There were remains of something in it. Rob shuddered. He noticed that there were degrees on the wall and a lot of expensive looking knick knacks as well as ten chess sets. One photo of the lawyer with the Mayor at some event. No other pictures of people. Miss Diliberto said, "that's strange."

"What's strange?"

"One of the chess sets is missing a black king."

Rob attended Carl Monroe's funeral; naturally it was raining. Since the deceased was being cremated, there was no necessity to stand under a drizzling umbrella. The short ceremony was held in a small room that appeared to be municipal and multifunctional. The eulogy was delivered by a minister of an unnamed Protestant sect. He presided efficiently over the small gathering; professional to the point of being almost robotic. Rob wondered who had hired him—maybe Carmen Diliberto—possibly the only person with any sort of a relationship with the attorney. Rob looked around at the mourners. He saw two ex-wives, several people who appeared to be local service people, several others who appeared to be lawyers and whose later conversations proved to Rob that his intuition was correct. There were no children and apparently no other relatives.

Rob overheard that Monroe had died intestate—ironic but typical for an attorney. Most of the lawyer mourners were family law attorneys. They didn't appear saddened by Monroe's passing. It appeared to Rob that many of them were relieved or reassured. Nothing overt. Just something in the air.

It was a strange group. They were professional and respectful; but one clique of attorneys seemed almost jovial. After several minutes, all the mourners headed methodically for the exit—almost as if responding to a silent signal. As they were approaching their cars, Rob noticed that a number of lawyers approached an attorney about to enter his black Lexus SUV. He was over six feet, dressed in a tailored navy pinstripe suit. No matter how you looked at him, he was a big guy. He smiled and extended his hand as each attorney greeted him. It resembled a receiving line. In fact, the manner in which many shook his hand looked more like congratulations than a farewell.

Rob intercepted a young attorney as she headed for her car, "If you don't mind my asking, who is that gentleman?"

"That's Tom Reagan," she continued her path as though that should be answer enough.

Rob took a couple of strides alongside her, "I'm sorry, I'm new here. Why are people shaking his hand like they're congratulating him?"

"They're just kidding."

"How so?"

"Well, a number of the family law practitioners didn't approve of Monroe's practice or his ethics."

"OK, why single out Mr. Reagan?"

"He was particularly outspoken about Monroe."

"So?"

"Reagan and Monroe had kind of a fierce rivalry…"

Rob stood aside and said, "Thanks."

When he left the funeral, he revisited a suppressed suspicion he had regarding the murder. Opposing attorneys. Rob's own experience through law school and his professional life indicated that attorneys weren't often hot-blooded. They were analytical and pragmatic. He couldn't visualize an attorney getting so emotional that he or she would commit murder for no apparent gain. Nor could he imagine a lawyer performing such a gruesome and precipitous act. He imagined that the gift of a Venus flytrap would be as far as they would go.

Nevertheless, he might look deeper into some of the attorneys.

The Patient Returns

Julie Harvey was a little anxious about her next meeting with The Patient. She knew that they were at a turning point. It could go in almost any direction, but she felt that they were on the first rung of a new ladder. While she wanted to leverage what could be a new openness, she was uneasy. Her own comfort level had been affected. She glanced anxiously at the clock that was always visible to both her and her patients. Although the professional S.O.P. was to hide the clock to avoid distracting patients with real-world temporal concerns during sessions, Julie permitted the awareness of time as an egalitarian symbol of shared session goals. All the patients had watches and phones anyway. She noticed that The Patient was late and began to wonder if she might never see The Patient again.

After revealing petty vandalism at the last session, The Patient recognized the insignificance and impotence of the act. The Patient wondered why it had taken so long to strike a real blow against the invaders to the area. Now it was two weeks later and the Patient wondered if Julie would connect the assassination at the work site with the act of vandalism. The Patient approached the psychologist's home office determined not to reveal this or any other act that might trigger a threat of exposure to a third party by the psychologist.

The Patient entered only nine minutes late and they exchanged greetings. They took their customary seats. "Well, did you analyze the consequences your action? Did it fix your issues with the work site?"

The Patient almost panicked and wondered briefly if Julie Harvey was referring to the shooting. Realizing that Ms. Harvey wouldn't handle such an extreme act so routinely, The Patient pretended that nothing had happened since the last session. "Yes, I have thought about it."

"How did it make you feel?"

No answer.

"What would you do differently?"

Still silence.

"Would you do it at all?"

The Patient adopted a bemused tone, "Maybe I was overreacting."

"Oh, how so?"

"What does it matter if I'm a few minutes late to work? I have to learn to relax and take things in stride."

Julie responded, "Do you think you can? I mean 'relax'."

"I don't see why not."

Julie let that hang in the air for a bit. Then leaned forward, "Let's review. A couple of weeks ago you told me that you broke the law. You didn't seem concerned that you could have gotten into a lot of trouble. Now you're all lattes and muffins and you're willing to forgive, forget, and go along to get along?"

The Patient sat motionless.

Julie sat just as still. The ticking of the clock on the coffee table became louder.

Finally, Julie said, "Let's look at this another way. If you got caught, would it make your situation worse, or better?"

The Patient leaned forward, "But that's the point, I didn't <u>get</u> caught."

"So you haven't told anyone? Absolutely no one? We've discussed that drinking is an issue. Are you sure that you never even hinted at this when you've been buzzed? Not with your drinking buddies?"

"No one" The Patient shifted in the seat, "Except you, Ms. Harvey."

The pause that followed was more than an awkward silence. If it had been a TV show, it would have been followed by a percussive and dramatic musical effect followed by a commercial break.

Julie broke the silence, "I appreciate your frankness. It's going to help us succeed in this therapy."

The Patient looked directly into Julie's eyes, "And you wouldn't tell anyone, would you?"

"Of course not. Not only wouldn't I, I can't."

"I've seen enough movies to know that priests and lawyers can't tell anyone in court what they've been told in confidence, but what about not in court? What about psychologists?"

"What you say here is sacrosanct, top secret. It's called *privileged communication*. Not only wouldn't I tell anyone. I can't. It's part of the oath of my profession. Only to prevent a certain crime am I permitted to say anything."

The Patient hesitated and then said, "If I mailed you a box and asked you to hold it for me and not to open it, would you?"

Julie nodded.

The patient continued, "And if I sent instructions with it, would you follow them?"

Julie replied, "Provided it wasn't anything illegal and wouldn't bring any harm to anyone, I would."

The Patient looked at the reflection of the desk clock on the glass top on the coffee table and said, "Well, that's good to know. I guess our time is up."

The Patient left. The psychologist sat for a while.

After one more patient, Julie Harvey took her usual walk with Siggy to the lighthouse. The lighthouse park was popular and usually crowded, but not today. It was mid-week, cloudy, and not yet the summer tourist season. The lighthouse attracted large numbers of tourists and sightseers during the season. Neither Julie nor her friends and neighbors could figure if it was the extraordinary ugliness of the structure itself or the beauty of the view from the prototypically rocky New England shore that attracted visitors. The lighthouse was a thin column tower that was purely and Puritanically utilitarian and industrial looking. It had no charm whatsoever—a sharp contrast to the islands and the historic colonial homes and mansions surrounding the sea views.

Right now the emptiness of the place afforded Julie an opportunity to be in the moment. She contemplated the views—the harbor on one side and the island-speckled Atlantic on the other side. The park was a perfect place to sit uninterrupted and work out the hidden feelings and thoughts scurrying around in her subconscious. She held out a dog biscuit, "Here, Siggy." The dog took the cookie appreciatively and settled down to chew. Then instead of finding a stick or begging for more, she sat in front of Julie and tilted her head inquisitively. "OK, girl, you can tell that something is nibbling at me? And not in a good way."

When no response was forthcoming from the animal, she said, "I suppose you mean that I should 'go with that feeling' and just say what's on my mind." She patted her pet's head, "I have this anxious feeling about one patient," she looked into Siggy's perpetually sympathetic eyes. "Of course, I'm always concerned about where or how they'll end up. Will they get off the dime? Experience greater happiness?" She watched the ripples in the gray-blue water for a couple of moments. She said, "But I have anxiety about the people around this patient. When I look into The Patient's eyes, I see anger and violence far greater than we ever discussed in sessions. When this patient asked me about privileged communications, I got the feeling that I was being assessed as a potential enemy or threat."

At that moment a voice said, "Are you a threat, Ms. Harvey?"

Julie turned. The Patient was standing behind her. Startled, she didn't answer for a moment. "What are you doing here?"

"Probably the same thing you are. Just cultivating inner harmony."

"Why haven't I ever seen you here before?"

The Patient took a step forward, displayed mock surprise and said, "I'm surprised to see you here as well. Do you come here often, Ms. Harvey?"

Julie remained silent for a moment while she deliberated whether she should answer. "You haven't answered my question. What I meant was 'do you come here often?'"

The Patient smiled, "Often enough."

After a long tense silence, The Patient did an about-face and ambled away. "You and your dog enjoy the day."

Julie and Siggy were suddenly alone.

When Julie Harvey arrived home, she found her door had been forced open. There was only one other sign of the intrusion. Her clock was shattered and turned face down on the coffee table.

She collapsed into her chair and patted Siggy at her side. She sat for an inordinate amount of time, weighing her own fears and suspicions against the potential benefits of the future counseling she might provide. Finally, she decided that since she had no further appointments scheduled with The Patient, she would wait to see what the Patient did. She would maintain her routine and watch for signs of danger. One part of her was secretly hoping that her relationship with this Patient was over.

Out on the Town

Kim made Rob's favorite dinner—spaghetti and sausage. Instead of wolfing it down enthusiastically as he usually did, Rob sat silent and almost sullen, slowly and listlessly twirling and eating forkfuls. "At this rate, Rob, you won't even have indigestion to remember the meal by. What's wrong?"

"Nothin'," Rob muttered.

"Nothin'," Kim muttered back in imitation. A long silence was finally broken when Kim said, "It's the hit-and-run, isn't it?"

When Rob just shrugged, Kim said, "How about if we hit-and-run? To a weekend in New York?"

Rob agreed.

They took off the next time Rob had his three day off-duty shift. They spent the day walking up and down Fifth Ave., wandering in and out of prestigious jewelry stores. As they left Tiffany's and Van Cleef & Arpels, they giggled like children at the way the clerks had stared at them, seeing right through their best apparel to their deficient bank books. They ate at a neighborhood deli of the kind New York is famous for, reveling as much in the towering hot pastrami sandwiches as in the insults with which they were served. Tired from their long walk, they retired to their hotel room in anticipation of a glorious evening out on the town—the planned climax of the weekend.

Despite, or maybe because of, their excitement about the weekend, Rob and Kim made love and fell asleep, exhausted from patrolling the city. Kim woke with a start. Shaking Rob, "Rob, Rob, oh my God, we're gonna be late for our reservations at Le Bernardi."

Rob blinked hard, grunted and jumped out of bed. He was already washing, grooming, and dressing as he blurted, "They won't hold them either." The whirlwind that Rob had become stopped, and he turned to notice that Kim was just staring at him. She was in total awe that he had overcome inertia and had progressed far beyond her in getting ready. Rob caught himself and sat down on the bed. They laughed in unison.

Kim checked the clock, "We have a half hour."

They finished dressing carefully and quietly. They had both brought their most fashionable clothes for the occasion. The kinds of clothes purchased for very special events that never seemed to occur. Back home on Boston's North Shore, they avoided getting dressed up. In fact, this trip was a major excuse to dress to the nines. For the Latrobes, it was the equivalent of dressing to the elevens.

As they were about to be seated in the restaurant, Rob became quiet and almost sullen as they gave the maitre d' their name. Kim studied Rob as they followed the maitre d' to their corner booth. There was a decided limp. As she sat down, Kim noted that Rob was wearing *two* left shoes. She smiled to herself through dinner, which was sinfully Epicurean, and Rob's spirits rose to match the occasion. Through cocktails, caviar, oysters, and a wonderful variety of unusual treats from the sea, extraordinary sides and salads, incomparably served, they chatted happily.

Finally, over coffee, just when Rob thought that his wife had been oblivious to his clumsy fashion faux pas, Kim asked, "So Rob, when did you decide to come to New York and teach these yokels about fashion?" Rob stared, his coffee cup halfway to his lips.

"I mean, two left shoes, from two different pairs—pretty suave!" From that point until the cab dropped them at their hotel room, Kim's comments ran the gamut from "Perfect for your dancing—two left feet" to "Will wearing the same gumshoes make detecting more soleful?" Once out of the cab, Rob did his Grandpa McCoy limp followed by his Lon Chaney Mummy foot drag into the hotel and up to the room.

"You should have been the detective. I realized my boo-boo when I was getting dressed to go out for our big night on the town. I thought I was really being subtle, but there's no fooling you, Sherlock!"

———<small>wooeroorooow</small>———

Rob and Kim returned from their trip to their former routine somewhat relaxed. Rob was nodding, fighting off sleep while he waited for Kim to come home on a boring Wednesday eve toward the end of the summer. He heard the garage door open and close. "Lucy, I'm home", Kim hollered with their traditional Desi Arnaz greeting.

Rob responded as always, "You got some 'splainin' to do." Kim put away her keys and joined Rob in the den.

She sighed and reported briefly on her day. "What about yours?"

Rob reacted with a shrug that implied that his day wasn't enjoyable or productive or that something was lacking. Kim prodded, "What's wrong?"

"I don't know...."

"Is it the damn hit-and-run again?"

"Not exactly."

"Then what?"

"You know I sat here most of the night while you were out with your friends. I tried to figure out the next step in the case. Why don't I have anyone who can help with the case? You don't usually let your off-days bring you down. You go out with your friends, hang out, and socialize. I don't even have any friends from work."

"Why don't you do something about it?"

"Such as..."

"I've been thinking about this for a while, Rob. I knew it sort of bothered me but until now, I didn't think it bothered you." Kim paused.

"Well?"

"OK, I want you to hear me out before you react." Rob smiled.

"It seems to me that there are two things that could be helpful." To lighten the mood, Kim enumerated her two points with gestures boldly out of sync a la Richard Nixon or a badly dubbed foreign movie, "First, you shouldn't be hanging around every night all by yourself with nothing to do but wait for me."

Rob's eyes showed his comprehension and his willingness to hear more. He made an obligatory attempt at denial, "Well I do play piano sometimes."

Kim plunged on, "Second, you need someone in law enforcement who you can share your concerns with. Someone to bounce ideas off."

"All right, but who and how?"

"A lot of the evenings I go out, it's informal—just a bunch of us getting together. Other times our office or one of the associations will hold an event for the express purpose of what you and I are discussing—socializing or networking, or just relief from work." Kim watched as Rob processed her ideas and decided it was time to let it develop.

Rob stood up and said, "You know I don't sound like much fun; all I really want to do is to show you a good time."

"Is that your mission?"

"I would be satisfied with that on my tombstone. Here lies Rob who showed Kim a good time."

Kim cocked her head to the side and said, "And that would be enough?"

"Yes. What do you want on your tombstone?"

She replied, "My tombstone will read, 'You call this a good time'?"

The next day Rob went to work, his mind preoccupied with the previous night's discussion. After working on briefs and having a discovery package assembled for the prosecution of a criminal fraud case, Rob took a break for lunch. He wandered over to the upscale cafeteria in the adjacent building. He returned with a salad and soup and entered the conference room that served as a break room. He passed by the bulletin board and stopped. He noticed a handbill that suddenly interested him:

Don't Pass the BAR—PARTY AT IT
One night only
All Members of Massachusetts Law Enforcement
Friends, Spouses, Fans and Other Supporters Are Welcome.
Admission = $30.
Includes:
One complimentary drink
Pass-around hors d'ouevres
Unlimited conversation and relaxation
No Felons or Defense Attorneys Allowed

It was followed by the date and time and the number to call and the option of signing up by email. Rob called the number, made the reservation, hung up, and dialed again, "Hi Kim, guess what I just did?"

———— ꙮꙮꙮꙮꙮꙮ ————

That same night, Dizzy parked her car, walked up her stairs, followed by the echo of her steps. Entering her house, she was greeted by the aroma of old coffee. She hollered "Daffy" knowing full well that her pet wouldn't respond. He was, after all, a cat. Like most cats, he felt he had to assert his feline haughtiness from time to time. She found him where he always was, sleeping on the foot of her bed. She removed her shoes, shuffled into the kitchen and poured some vodka over ice. She didn't take time for shaking, stirring, vermouth, or olives; she just wanted to sit and focus on the Parker case. Try as she might, no ideas or revelations came to her. She picked up her Lehane mystery and listened to Gene Harris with the Ray Brown Trio on her iPod. Two of the best together, piano and bass gave her a chance for relaxation or inspiration. Either one would be just what she needed.

Less than an hour later she went to bed. As always, she took something to help her sleep. She noticed the large number of old and out-of-date and out-of-need medications lined up in her bathroom cabinet. They were totems—a paean to ancient superstitions—she feared that throwing them out might endanger her future health. She puzzled over the case. It would call for a rare combination of thoroughness and creativity—build the box very carefully and then less carefully think out of it.

She had no idea how far out of it she would go.

On Her Own

They had been married for eighteen years, but to Carolyn she and Larry had always been together, especially as part of a longstanding small community. From occasional vacations to camping and hiking to music to drinking—their friends hung out together.

Carolyn knew that one of the attributes that drew Larry to her was her toughness. She had a durability, resilience and strength that Larry found interesting and sometimes challenging. Whether it was fighting the elements while hiking, disputing a charge from the bank, or asserting her political opinions, Carolyn could be tenacious, even ferocious. It was this toughness that allowed her to enjoy Larry's entertaining antics and to withstand his varying moods. While she and Larry were together, they always looked out for each other. They enjoyed each other, but over time they found it difficult to make the marriage work. Something was missing. Maybe love. Finally, as a practical matter, Carolyn determined to end the marriage.

She sought out a divorce attorney, most of whom referred to themselves either accurately or euphemistically as family law attorneys. Although she didn't anticipate the dissolution of her marriage to be "a federal case," she wanted to get through it as quickly as possible without giving up too much. She was aware of the importance of the step and wanted to avoid making a mistake that could cost her dearly at some future date.

Carolyn appreciated the directness of a local lawyer who called himself a divorce attorney. Carl Monroe had quite a reputation; the financial success it had obtained was obvious the minute Carolyn entered his office. She noted the art adorning the walls, the tasteful and professionally selected appointments. When she received her final bill, she understood first-hand how it had all been paid for. She had thought that her retainer (no measly sum) would cover the costs of her simple, straightforward case. After months of delay that Monroe attributed to a capricious court system, charges mounted up.

The divorce proceedings had been an ordeal, but Carolyn looked anxiously forward to Life Without Larry. However, as her kids grew, she had to get a job and figure out a way to take care of them. Larry had been of little help with the childcare except for his income and as a "wait 'til Daddy gets home" threat for discipline. That they hadn't really collaborated as parents was one of the ruptures that eventually contributed to the dissipation of the marriage. Although she had been raising her children primarily on her own, the task promised to be more daunting now. She was reassured that her mother would be happy to take care of her grandchildren. Her best friend and some of the other parents would also help her until she could arrange for reliable and affordable childcare.

Now Carolyn had to get a job. She pared her requirements to three elements. First, it had to be something she wouldn't mind doing. Second, it had to be a job that required her skills and affinities. Finally she had to be able to start right away. As a single mom, she couldn't afford to be out of work financially or psychologically. She had worked in the insurance industry for good money, but it bored her. In any case, career paths and high compensation would take a back seat at this juncture.

She liked to cook and bake and enjoyed interpersonal contact. So she started looking at the food service venues in her area—restaurants, diners, coffee shops, even convenience stores. Since they had high turnover, she might be able to find an opening. Carolyn would check them out in the morning and then return in the afternoon to those sites (not many) that had an opening or those where she thought she would really like to work and could bring something to the table (literally and figuratively). She visited ten stores the first morning and sat (or loitered) and observed as much as possible. That afternoon she revisited three, putting in an application to one, although there were no openings at the moment. The pattern repeated for almost a week. Either out of desperation or wishful thinking, Carolyn decided to try Bar None. After all, she certainly knew the place and the clientele. In the morning it wasn't open for business, but the doors were open. She entered, walked up to the bar, leaned over it, waited and sang out "Hello?" She heard shuffling behind her and turned to find her ex-brother-in-law standing behind her. He said, "Hello Carolyn, what are you doing here?"

In her anxiety to find work and her desire for familiar surroundings, she had overlooked the fact that Keith worked here. His tone was cold and professional, and she thought she detected a grace note of hostility. Or maybe she just felt guilty because she hadn't seen him since before the divorce.

"I'm looking for work. I have to support my kids."

"Isn't Larry helping out?"

"He pays child support, but…."

Keith paused, began to say something, and finally sighed, "We don't have any openings. I don't think it would be a good idea for you to work here." He turned and walked away. Carolyn left.

Two doors down, she visited her favorite coffee shop/bakery to relax and have a cup of coffee. As she sat down, she began to look at the little café differently. She saw delicious-looking muffins, cookies, scones, and pastries in the display cabinet, a couple of young women taking orders and serving hot, aroma-suffused coffee. As it always was, the place was crowded—bustling at a steady and manageable pace. The shop was about to close for the day when all the servers adjourned to a back room. She heard applause and cheering. She waited until one of the counter people emerged and explained, "Sorry for leaving you alone, but one of the bakers is moving away and today is her last day. It's kind of sudden so we're giving her a send-off."

"I'll be leaving in a second." Then Carolyn's eyes widened and she turned toward the baker, "Does that mean that there's an opening?"

Party Time

Rob's commitment to attend the Bar Party was coming due. His sense of duty or guilt (which was which?) compelled him to begin to regret his commitment. First Manhattan and now a party. How much R & R could a civil servant take?

By the time the day of the party rolled around, Rob was surprised to find himself looking forward to it. He prepared to leave in time to arrive a half hour after the starting time. His preparation consisted of removing his tie and unbuttoning his shirt—a little wild and crazy for Rob the Professional, but he was willing.

He arrived at the bar shortly after the party was scheduled to start. He gave his old blue Toyota to valet parking, determined not to be embarrassed by all the surrounding Lexuses and BMW's. He had been to the restaurant on several previous occasions. It was one of those that bordered Quincy Market and Boston's Italian North End. It was dark with dim old-fashioned lights and rough-hewn woodwork and floors, polished only by age. It was so conspicuously colonial that he began to look for Redcoats, muskets, and patriots with tri-corner hats. What he found instead was a wait staff in blouses and dress corsets. Close enough. A sign on a placard said "private party." He followed it and recited his name to the welcoming hostess who crossed him off a list, and presented him with a name badge and a red ticket. She stamped his hand, "The red ticket is for your complimentary drink; go right in, counselor, and enjoy yourself."

The room was filled with a number of familiar "suits," some of whom he waved to. Everybody had a drink in one hand. Being a little anxious, he ordered a martini from one waitress and grabbed a scallop wrapped in bacon from another. The server took his ticket and moved on. He slowly meandered over to one end of the bar where he could observe the scene. Mingling wasn't his thing. The martini was perfect and as he sipped it and began to relax, he concentrated on the party. It had been a long time since he had attended a professional social gathering; he analyzed the group from his sideline vantage point.

The crowd was mostly male, various ages, with a few females mixed in. Suits were mixed in with police uniforms and a few casually dressed guests. He took another sip and became aware that he shared his small spot on the periphery with another attendee. He slowly turned toward the presence and the other attendee turned toward him. He was staring into very black eyes in a smiling face—belonging to a well-dressed black woman. Rob thought that there was something about her demeanor led that suggested law enforcement rather than law practice—a cop. If she was plain clothes, there was nothing plain about her; she wore a bright powder blue ascot and a tailored navy suit that was perfect for her figure—which was also perfect. Her name tag read "Dahlia Gillespie."

It took a second for it to register. While they had communicated in several ways, they had never met each other.

She read his tag and offered her hand, "Hi Mr. Latrobe."

"Hi, Ms. Gillespie. Or should I say 'Detective'?"

"Well, since this is a social occasion, you can call me 'Dizzy'."

Rob chuckled, "It's about time we met in person. Our schedules never mesh. So Dizzy. Do you play trumpet or have balance issues?"

"No, I just think that the name sticks, you know?" She smiled broadly. "My friends call me 'Rob'."

"Does that have anything to do with larceny?"

Rob laughed. He knew they were going to get along.

They found a table top and took their drinks there. They discussed the real Dizzy Gillespie and bebop and a few movies about jazz. They noted

Clint Eastwood's classic <u>Bird</u> and Woody Allen's funny and tragic <u>Sweet and Low Down</u>. Forest Whittaker and Sean Penn had really nailed their roles. Dizzy was a more intense fan, but Rob was a sometime musician and got his kicks from playing jazz keyboards, primarily for himself.

Rob ordered another round for the two of them. "Maybe I should order a Black Dahlia in honor of your given name."

"That's my name, and I'm aware of the flower, but I've never heard of the drink. What is it?"

"It was named after the title character in a Raymond Chandler screenplay as well as the victim of an infamous Los Angeles murder. It's made with ice, vanilla vodka, black raspberry liqueur, coffee liqueur and a slice of orange. I really don't have much drinking knowledge but I love mysteries."

"Raymond Chandler? I love him. And, in fact, I love all detective stories!"

The next hour was spent discussing detective novels and movies they both enjoyed. The talk of movies and books had allowed them to keep the conversation light. The event was supposed to allow professionals to relax and become better acquainted with their associates.

They both wanted to leave before 11:00 and at 10:30 they departed, saying good night and promising to discuss the sniper case at 5:00 the following afternoon.

Two Heads

Rob arrived fifteen minutes early for the 5:00 meeting with Dizzy at a designated bar in the Seaport district of Boston. He waited at a small table with a view of the entrance. Rob watched Dizzy approach. He imagined her as the heroine of a detective novel. She still had a nice figure and moved gracefully, comfortably aware of her environment. She joined him and ordered vodka on ice while he ordered a dry Tito's martini. As they shared some appetizers, they filled in personal details—their education, training, marital status. Dizzy commented, "So we agree that you're happily married and I'm happily unmarried, shall we review the Parker case?"

"Just one question first. I know why I'm happily married, but I don't understand why you're not."

Dizzy smiled, "I never found the right guy."

"Never? Not even close?"

"There was one guy...."

"So?"

Dizzy sipped her drink, savoring it—and maybe a memory. "We were serious for about two years. He was funny, considerate, and kind. He was also very intelligent and talented. But...."

Rob said, "I think I know what the problem was. What did he look like?" Rob was certain that someone as perfect as this guy was and hadn't been the "right guy" must have looked like Freddie Kruger or worse. It was all that was left.

Dizzy thought for a second. "Sort of like Bradley Cooper except...."
Rob waited expectantly. "Except?"
Dizzy answered "Except he was taller."

Rob chuckled out loud. For some reason, the comment really cracked Rob up. He explained, "The fatal flaw in this guy was that he was handsome—and tall."

Dizzy looked at him unblinking. Once again Rob decided that he would never understand women. To move the subject toward work, Rob raised his glass and toasted, "Here's to perfect martinis and imperfect men."

Dizzy clinked her glass on his and said, "Here's to perfect martinis."

"OK," said Rob, "from martinis to murder. I've received all your reports and summaries on the shooting and I've sent you all the pertinent forensic and database information. "What I'd really appreciate is hearing your take, including nuances and intuition—the stuff that doesn't make it into reports."

"So far the only progress I've been able to achieve is to tentatively eliminate some areas. I don't think that the wife did it. It doesn't seem that co-workers or neighbors have any idea of how, why or who killed Jack Parker."

"No one who could benefit from his death?"

"No life insurance or property windfall and no enemies that I could discover."

"And no witnesses."

"None. But I plan to return to the area. It's just a feeling, but I think there's something to be learned there. I don't usually rely on gut, but so far there are no real clues."

"How can I help?"

"Right now there's no case to build, no witnesses, no suspects. So I can try to move forward by legwork."

"And know that I'm there to help. To actively support or act as a sounding board until we get further. What's your next step?"

Dizzy finished her drink and started to leave. "I'll head back to the area of the crime scene. I still hold out hope that someone might have seen something that could shed light but they didn't really realize it. And there's a neighbor I'm looking forward to finding more about."

"Who is?"

"A blogger extraordinaire."

X Rated

The incomplete building showed no signs of progress, but Dizzy hoped that her investigation might. She was no sooner in the building than she began to recall that feeling of not being alone. She could see from end to end on the floor she was on, so she took the open stairwell to explore the next floor. As she turned the corner, she heard movement and the sound of glass. "Who's there?" She moved quickly, her hand on her pistol and ready. Her attention was directed to a large column at the opposite stairwell. Suddenly, an object rolled out; it looked almost like a hand grenade. Dizzy hesitated and then advanced quickly but cautiously. It was a small empty liquor bottle—Jack Daniel's. A little embarrassed, she removed her hand from her pistol and proceeded to the office building.

Dizzy entered the blogger's one room office. The walls were adorned with printed graffiti, posters, and newspaper headlines. Dizzy found an angry young man in the person of Francis X. Bryan seated in the center. She greeted him and identified herself.

He responded, "Most people call me 'X'".

"X, why do you think the worker was murdered?"

The blogger announced, "Murder? More like an assassination. These municipal despots are just as bad as the state and federal governments. They use our tax dollars to put us out of business. We have no recourse, no defense…"

Just then the door to his office opened and one of the most handsome men Dizzy had seen in a long time entered. Dizzy was thankful for the interruption as well as the treat for her eyes. The newcomer looked at Dizzy nervously and then at X, "I'll come back later." He backed out and closed the door.

Dizzy searched X's face for an explanation. "That's just Dan. He does contract work for the IT business down the hall and sometimes drops by."

"Oh? Dan who?"

"Dan Daniels. Nice guy. Actually pretty funny."

Dizzy jotted down the name and reluctantly returned to the rant which lasted off and on for almost another hour. Despite the vehemence of the outburst, Dizzy couldn't decide if X sympathized with the shooter or the victim. She left, feeling that X was a little extreme, but he certainly didn't "mark the spot". His quirky manner rendered him an unlikely suspect in a shooting requiring such precision. Moreover, X had no real insights as a witness. She would have to put this excursion in the "waste of time" column. Except. Except for the visitor named Dan Daniels. There was something more furtive about him than the usual skittishness Dizzy encountered as an investigator. She was almost certain he was hiding something. Dizzy never placed much stock in hunches. In fact, she had never really had one. Until now. She determined to find out more about Dan Daniels.

Two for the Road

"I have some good news and some bad news. Which do you want to hear first?

It was ADA Latrobe. Dizzy said, "OK, give me the good news first."

"You and I have been assigned another case."

"And the bad news?"

"You and I have been assigned another case."

"What kind of case?"

"A homicide."

Rob explained, "It's a hit-and-run, and I have no idea where to start or what to do in this case. Until we apprehend someone, I don't know what the crime is. Is it manslaughter? Murder one? Murder two?"

Dizzy said, "But you have a suspect."

"I don't have a suspect."

"Do you have a victim?"

"Of course, I have a victim. And I have witnesses—but they can't identify the perpetrator or the vehicle. Other than to say that it was a black SUV."

Dizzy said, "Rob, working with you is just good news. Whose idea was it?"

"I'm glad you feel that way. It was my idea. I caught the case and had to pick a detective."

"You seem frustrated. You may not know the legal nature of the crime, but you have some advantages. In some ways your case is simpler than most homicides.

Rob was intrigued. He went on to summarize the known facts so Dizzy could explain her perspective.

"You have the advantage of knowing the real identity of the victim. And you know how and when and where the homicide took place. What you don't know is the same as most murder investigations. You don't know who committed the crime or why. In other words, you have the body, no suspects. Other than the obviously brilliant maneuver of assigning me, what have you done so far?"

"Checked out the crime scene, went to the ME."

Dizzy interrupted, "McCann?"

"Yes."

Dizzy cringed slightly. "Since the victim was killed near his law office at the end of the work day, we might focus the scope of the investigation on his work life. At least at the start."

"It would make sense that an attorney might have serious enemies."

"Especially a litigator."

"Especially a divorce attorney. How many divorced people have good things to say about their attorney or the process?"

Rob said, "So I guess I start by checking out Monroe's recent cases, ask a few questions, learn more about him."

Dizzy did what in another context would have been a perfect double-take. "Did you say Monroe? Carl Monroe?"

"You knew him?"

"Dizzy paused, "Not exactly. I was investigating the Parker shooting, interviewing people in the vicinity. I was at a law firm and one of the partners was talking about our Mr. Monroe...in a not entirely complimentary way. Monroe really pissed this guy off."

"Why?"

"Apparently unethical. At least some attorneys thought he was."

Rob wondered, "I wonder how his clients felt."

"Maybe you should be looking for pissed off clients."

Dizzy left on that suggestion. Rob followed, wondering if the missing chess piece was important enough or even a clue to have mentioned. It was a little creepy. A few minutes later Rob had a second creepy experience when he noticed a man surreptitiously watching him. Rob turned away and when he turned back, the man was gone. Rob's only remaining impression of him was that he was unusually good-looking.

Julie Harvey waited nervously. The Patient was her next appointment. Other than an email to set the appointment, they had had no contact since they had met at the park. She had felt threatened at the park and finding her clock mysteriously broken didn't ease her misgivings. She didn't know if it was coincidence or not, but the clock had stopped at 3:00, the time for The Patient's standing appointment. She was fearful enough that she broke her rule and had her dog stay with her in the office. When the Patient was almost fifteen minutes late, she dialed the number she had on file. No answer. The hour went by. No Patient.

Ever again.

Re: Monroe

While he worked on other matters, Rob assigned a legal assistant to check out the hit-and-run victim's recent cases. "Let's look at his most recent cases and see if can find clients who were unhappy with fees, or irritated or unhappy with the results. Call them directly if you have to. Claim that you're looking for references."

Two days later, Rob found a list on his desk. It contained a summary of twelve of Carl Monroe's clients going back two and a half years. The Word document covering the two pages read:

Rob,

> *You requested a list of Carl Monroe's recent cases where clients might possibly be unhappy with his services. Privileged communications made it almost impossible for us to view the actual details, so I relied on public information and those client "references." The clients were understandably reluctant to speak even when I assured anonymity. I looked for the following:*

> - *Complaints, peer review, anecdotal material when they were willing*
> - *Longest duration of litigation*

- *Most volatile issue based on public records*
- *Mention of anger in media coverage*

Good luck and keep the faith,
Your loyal servant
Melissa Brown

Before attacking the list of people involved with Monroe, Rob took one more shot at finding a witness to the accident itself. There was a small store wedged in between the retailers on the street where the hit-and-run took place. Of all things, it was a cobbler. Rob smiled to himself as he recalled his footwear fiasco in New York. Muttering to himself "the game's afoot", he approached the tiny shop shoehorned between the bank and a real estate office. An old-fashioned wooden sign hung crookedly above the door. A chime announced Rob's entry. The store was an anachronism, a souvenir from a much simpler time. Rob looked around while he waited for the proprietor to make an appearance. Dimly lit and profusely littered, every surface held a shoe or part of one. Shoes were everywhere and the not unpleasant odor of leather and shoe polish permeated the place. Just as Rob was about to holler a greeting, a short, round graying man appeared. He could have been Geppetto's twin. He reminded Rob of S. Z. Sakall, the lovable character actor nicknamed "Cuddles" in Casablanca. When he spoke, his thick Russian accent was right out of Boris Badenov. He looked over his rimless glasses at Rob, "May I help you? I am the world's best cobbler."

"Hi Mr.......?"

"Davidoff, Alexander Davidoff."

"Mr. Davidoff, I was wondering if you saw the hit-and-run the other day or if you knew the victim, Carl Monroe."

The cobbler didn't register any surprise or affect from the information. But he had a twinkle in his eye, "See it? No, I didn't see anything."

"Did you know the victim?"

"Not exactly." He paused, and pointed in the air. He disappeared for a few seconds and returned with a pair of boots, "These are his."

Rob was looking at a pair of very costly-looking reddish boots, obviously made from some sort of reptile skin. He looked questioningly at the cobbler. "Nice boots. Do they tell you anything about him?"

The diminutive tradesman smacked his lips, a little reluctant to speculate. "Well, I can tell you about his footwear. They are Lucchese hand-cut hornback head boots made from American alligators."

"Are they expensive?"

"Among the most expensive money can buy."

"How much?"

"About $5000. Would you like to buy them?"

Rob quipped, "I would, but they're not my size."

Just then the cobbler looked up at the door which was open to the street. As a German Shepard came in, the cobbler brought out dog biscuits and fed them to the pet. He waved to the dog's owner. It was obviously part of a routine

When the cobbler's attention returned, Rob asked, "What kind of man spends that much on footwear?"

"The same kind who doesn't care about endangered species," responded the cobbler.

Rob left the store thinking about character—how people could be starkly different beneath their surface images. For example, Carl Monroe seemed to be the stereotypical shyster lawyer. No redeeming value. The cobbler, on the other hand, was a kindly, affable good man, concerned with, among other things, endangered species. Yet, here was the cobbler trading in cowhide and other leather, considered by environmentalists to be a major factor in endangering wildlife and part of the cruel treatment of hide-bearing animals. So how deep did one have to dive to find true character? Could the killer appear to be something other than what he was? Would Rob recognize him if he saw him?

He decided to drop by Monroe's office for another look. He found Carmen Diliberto boxing up the remaining items from Monroe's office.

They exchanged greetings and as he moved a box for her to a pyramid of similar boxes on the side, he asked "How are you doing, Ms. Diliberto?" She appeared sadder but more relaxed than when they had met.

"Okay, I guess," she responded.

"Where are the boxes going?"

"To Carl's, Mr. Monroe's house."

"I've been there, nice house, more like a museum than a house. Doesn't look lived-in, but it has lots of nice things."

"You mean expensive things?"

Rob nodded.

"Carl didn't like much, didn't do much. Except acquire things. He'd buy clothes, fishing gear, guns, etc. and never really do anything with them. The joy was in the acquisition for Carl."

"Who gets his files?"

Carmen stopped moving things for the first time. She had been perpetual motion since Rob entered. She slowly surveyed the room and said, "That's the thing. The probate court will have to figure it out."

"What are you going to do now?"

"I'll go work for 'Elena Kagan' Reagan, the enemy."

"Who?"

"Tom Reagan, a partner at Walker, Reagan, and Esposito. Another litigation firm in the area. Reagan is a family law attorney."

"Why there?"

"Because I can. I know the local family courts and I understand which tactics pay off." She thought for a second, "Reagan was Carl's arch rival and Carl won more often than not, and almost certainly made more money. I think Walker Reagan would like some of that over there."

"Why do you want to go there?"

Diliberto looked Rob in the eyes, "Not a lot of choices. I can put my skills and knowledge to use there. Besides, I always felt that Reagan was a more ethical professional."

Rob ventured, "Did Monroe have any redeeming features or scruples?"

"He served on a couple of non-profit boards and donated generously on occasion."

"One more question. Why is Tom Reagan named after the Supreme Court Justice Elena Kagn?"

"'Cause it rhymes."

Rob asked for a business card from Diliberto's destination firm.

He returned to his office and the prepared list of Monroe's clients. His interviews revealed that some clients were unhappy and many were particularly unhappy with Monroe. They thought he was arrogant, if not unscrupulous. This dissatisfaction was prevalent whether they were male or female or had won or lost their cases. Their attitudes ranged from anger and sadness to relief. Some were taciturn while others were downright gabby, probably reflecting an adjustment to loneliness. Finally, at what would almost certainly be his last pre-arranged interview, Rob rang the doorbell under the name of Carolyn Johnston. The name Gallon had been crossed out. He was greeted by a good-looking woman dressed in a white blouse and jeans. They sat in the living room and she poured two mugs of coffee.

Rob noticed that Carolyn was in great shape and seemed calm. He realized that most of the divorcees he had met appeared to be "in the pink" despite (or because of?) their divorces. He leaned back and relaxed. Although he wasn't likely to unearth any important or relevant information about Carl Monroe, he was giving it the old college try. The interview became more of a natural conversation than an interview.

"How did you happen to pick Carl Monroe as your attorney?"

Carolyn's eyes moved slightly upward, "It seems like overkill now, but I wanted an attorney who would never waver from a divorce—and would get me as much as possible so I could carry on as a single mom."

"Why, do a lot of attorneys 'waver'?"

Carolyn leaned forward, "Some try to compromise or even mediate, but Carl had a reputation for aggressive litigation."

"Ms. Johnston, if you don't mind my asking, why did you decide to divorce? What was your husband like?"

She sat back, "It wasn't any one thing. We had grown apart. Larry seemed to be more alive at work and began to spend more time with his friends and his brother. He had become quiet and remote at home. I realized that I didn't miss him when he wasn't here. When I pondered the future, I realized that my husband wasn't a positive or important part of it. So separating seemed to be the right thing to do."

"Were you happy with the result? With your attorney?"

She exhaled, "All in all, yes. There were times when I thought he was inflating his billing hours, but I'm sure he got me everything he could."

"If you don't mind my asking, does that mean that you received a reasonable settlement?"

"It was adequate. But my ex and his family were outraged. I suppose that's usually the way it is, but I still had to get a job at the bakery and coffee shop around the corner."

"How did you feel when you heard Monroe had died?"

"I'm not sure. He was young and it was so sudden... I felt kind of bad."

"Thank you," Rob stood up to leave. Carolyn accompanied him to the door. "I never asked you why the Attorney General's office is interested in a hit-and-run. Do you think it was murder?" Rob answered truthfully that hit-and-run cases were often investigated by a state commission. "Why do you ask?"

"I think that a lot of his adversaries genuinely hated him. And there were rumors that he had affairs with some of his female clients."

Rob delayed his question long enough to avoid being prying or inquisitional, "Did he...?"

Carolyn's response was immediate, "He flirted and hinted, but I put the warning sign up right away."

Rob thanked her and left, but he felt that his picture of Carl Monroe and his client relationships had been painted only in broad strokes. He wondered where else he could gain an insight into Carl Monroe's professional life. If it was a targeted hit-and-run, Monroe must have pissed somebody off. He walked to his car, thinking Reagan's name had appeared too many times not to be questioned. He and Carl Monroe seemed somehow joined at the hip—or at least the gavel. He took out the business card he had taken from Monroe's former assistant. He called Walker, Reagan, and Esposito.

Rob entered the somewhat imposing law office, gave his card to the receptionist. He was ten minutes early and sat in the reception area. As he waited, he wondered how his life would be if he had chased the compensation offered by a private firm like this. He recognized that his life would be indeed different—not necessarily better. He liked the feeling of supporting the system, enforcing laws. He heard his name and looked up into the beautiful green eyes of a well-dressed woman who could only have been Reagan's assistant. He followed her into Reagan's office, rejected an offer of coffee and sat down. "Thank you for seeing me on such short notice, Mr. Reagan."

"Not a problem. Call me Tom."

Rob looked around the office so as not to stare or to appear to be examining his host, "Call me Rob." This was the same charismatic gentleman he had seen receiving salutations if not congratulations at Carl Monroe's funeral.

"How can I help? Is this about the unfortunate killing down there?" he gestured toward the work site.

"No, it's about the unfortunate death of Carl Monroe."

"Oh?"

"You knew him pretty well, didn't you?"

"Not really. I saw him in court periodically but never had any personal conversations with him."

"So if you don't mind my asking, why did you attend his funeral?"

Reagan hesitated, surprised that ADA Latrobe was aware of his presence at the event. He said, "I was kind of representing a number of family law attorneys; we thought somebody in our special practice area should be there."

Rob asked, "It almost looked like you were sharing some joy with some other colleagues, celebrating."

Reagan thought for a moment, then said, "You must be talking about a kind of sarcastic festive moment; they were kidding me because Carl Monroe was a pain in the ass, and I had been more vocal than others in saying so."

"But you never really spent any time with him? Other than in court?"

"That's correct. Other than some negotiations, usually with our clients present."

"You have anything to add?"

Reagan rose and shook hands with Rob. "No. I hope I've been some help."

As Rob left the law firm, he passed a small office with its door open. The young man behind the desk looked up and watched Rob. As Rob waited in the hall for the elevator, he noticed that the man advanced to his doorway. He had intense blue eyes.

Rob got off the elevator and walked next door to a small coffee shop. He wanted a short 'time out" to think about the case. He brought a cup of dark roast in a ceramic mug to a small table and sat down. Two sips later, the man with the curious blue eyes entered the shop and walked over. "Do you mind if I sit here?" Rob gestured to the seat.

The young man sat. He said, "I bet you're here to investigate the public works shooting."

"What makes you say that?"

"You look like an investigator, you visited that law firm, and nothing much else happens around here," Francis X. Bryan gave his business card to Rob.

Rob read it and said, "So you must know what's going on around here, Mr. Bryan?"

"You could say that."

"What if I told you that I'm investigating the death of an attorney?" Rob had not offered ID, keeping Bryan curious.

"Which attorney?"

"Carl Monroe. Next town over."

"I heard about that. Hit-and-run."

"What else have you heard?"

"Not much...."

"Did you know Mr. Monroe by sight?"

"Yes, I saw his photo in the paper and online when he died."

"Was he ever around here?"

"It's funny you should ask. I saw him several times with Mr. Reagan."

If Rob had physical antennae, they would have risen right out of his head. "Where? What were they doing?"

Proud of his apparently surprising information, Bryan elaborated, "I have some interesting theories about that."

Rob waited.

"Well, I've seen the two of them several times. They were on a bench in the corner of a small park that no one visits. I happened to kind of follow Reagan one day when he left the building without his briefcase and not dressed for court. They definitely didn't want to be seen together. The meeting wasn't social or casual. I saw them two other times from a distance so they couldn't see me. What do you think they could be conspiring about?

"I have no idea. You're the one who saw them. What do you think?"

"Let's see. They're both divorce attorneys. Face each other a lot. What if they're figuring out how to extend their cases? Instead of trying to settle, they're agreeing to milk their clients for all they can."

"Interesting, Mr. Bryan. Do you have any proof?"

"No, they're too clever."

"Do you see any motive or indication of murder in this?"

Bryan was silent. Rob nodded and left.

The next morning Rob rounded the corner and jogged the last stretch at an easy pace. He always enjoyed running—in almost any form— sports, races, as well as a rare triathlon. Over the last several years he had substituted or supplemented running with cross-country skiing, snowshoeing, and bike riding. Even now with his work load at an all-time high, he managed to maintain most of his workout routine.

He loped, stopped, and stretched and then opened his door. He walked into the kitchen where Kim was seated, munching on a bagel and sipping coffee. Rob splashed his face with water, poured coffee and sat across from his wife. It was the weekend and she was still in her bathrobe. Seeing this as an opportunity for a conversation, Rob asked, "What are you up to today?"

"I've got some returns to make."

"Returns again?"

"Yes, I've been searching for an outfit."

"You're on another 'mission from God'?"

Kim glared, and then her gaze softened to playful.

"Is this one of those deals where you come back with more clothes than you left with, but you still call it a return?"

"Maybe...."

Rob thought it would be wonderful if were this successful extracting confessions from suspects or witnesses. He adjusted ion his seat and faced Kim, "Can we talk about something serious?"

Kim pushed her coffee mug to the side. "Sure. What about?"

"Divorce."

Target Practice

When Keith got an idea, he was a little like a runaway drone—there was no holding him back. He and Larry had always been interested in firearms, evolving from cowboys and Indians and toy guns as youngsters to a real hobby for Keith as a grownup. He had a permit and owned both a Smith & Wesson .357 Magnum and a Ruger hunting rifle with a scope. The Magnum was inspired by Clint Eastwood, or more accurately, by Dirty Harry. The Ruger by its accuracy. The irony of his hobby was that Keith hiked, but he didn't hunt. Larry would say in a sing song tone, that Keith "didn't want to hurt the itty bitty animals."

Keith decided that he wanted to look for a new weapon at the gun show making its annual visit to the region. That Larry would accompany him was almost a given. They asked Sheryl to join them. She not only agreed to go with them, she shared a previously unrevealed interest. "I'm glad you asked. I'm interested in finding out about pistols." As they often did when embarking on an activity, the three vigorously raised their right thumbs.

The gun show resembled a car or boat show and it attracted an astonishingly large number of serious enthusiasts. Masses of people—young, old, families, groups and individuals, and mostly males were crowded armpit to armpit. They socialized with others who shared their unusual hobby as they explored and shopped—sort of a reunion over weapons instead of yearbooks.

After waiting in line for almost an hour to gain admission, the trio became part of the throng of attendees. They investigated pistols, rifles, semi-automatic weapons, shotguns, knives, camos, crossbows, ammo, and accessories—brand new, historic, and antique. Some exhibitions took on a museum-like atmosphere.

The trio gawked at pistols—small derringers, antique dueling pistols, long-barreled revolvers, machine pistols and more. An outsized switchblade sporting a gargantuan blade three feet long was one of the most memorable of the odd and historic weapons.

The brothers and Sheryl wandered and explored for the better part of an hour. They saw hundreds of fascinating and tempting items. They made no major purchases. They decided that Keith should be content with what he already had. Larry knew where Keith kept his hunting rifle and could borrow it whenever he wanted.

They had satisfied their curiosity and agreed to find Sheryl so they could leave. Larry said, "When I last saw her she was at an exhibit of movie props and reproductions." They set off in the general direction of where they had last seen her. The brothers approached quietly and watched Sheryl examine a weird and vicious looking dagger. It was almost two feet long from end to end. The handle featured a faux ruby, and the blade was curved, canted, and sharp-pointed. The sign read, "Valyrian Steel Cat's Paw Dagger." The card underneath continued, "Replica of Game of Thrones prop—left at the scene of an attempted assassination of Bran Stark." They were pondering the purchase when Sheryl turned and said, "I want to buy a gun."

The Gallons brothers stopped in their tracks and looked at Sheryl with some surprise.

"Oh? Any gun in particular?" asked Keith.

Larry asked, "Do you have a gun permit?"

"No, I don't."

Keith said, "If you buy a gun at the show, you can apply for a permit there."

Larry chimed in, "You can get a permit even if you don't buy a gun."

Sheryl said, "I'll be counting on you guys to advise me. I like this one." She pointed to a .38 Colt Cobra. It was small and hammerless. "It looks like it would fit in my purse like a glove."

At this point, the salesman behind the counter saw she had real interest and quietly took it out and handed it to her. Sheryl hefted the pistol and aimed it at the counter.

She turned to the salesman and commented, "It's much lighter than I expected."

The salesman said, "You won't find many pistols lighter or easier to fire; it has no hammer." As Sheryl studied the weapon, he continued, "This is the same gun that Jack Ruby used to kill Lee Harvey Oswald."

"How much is it?" Larry asked.

"Jack Ruby's gun last sold for $220,000."

Keith broke in, "How much is THIS one?"

The seller looked at Sheryl, "Are you interested?"

Sheryl ended up buying the gun for $240."

Violent Exchange

The sun had gone down on a beautiful day when the Devil's Jury regulars began to straggle into Bar None for what promised to be a typical evening of social repartee. As usual, individuals exchanged greetings and some reports of their day's events. Keith and Dan listened as Sheryl related to Larry her encounter with the car that threatened her earlier in the week. So Dan suggested that the Jury members should each describe a violent incident they had either participated in or witnessed.

Dan glanced around the table and Ben, who looked like the least violent person at the table, related a story of road rage:

"This guy pulled alongside me. He had been beeping at me. He asked why I was driving so slowly. I told him I was trying to get my dicks in a row."

Dan and Keith looked at each other, recognizing that Ben had actually said "dicks" instead of "ducks".

"He got all pissed off and he yells at me to 'go fly a kike'. I'm not violent but I don't tolerate anti-Semitism. I flipped him the turd and took off. He follows me and tries to slam into my car. I was sweating buckets, didn't know what to do. I drove past as quick as I could. He tailgated my car and tried to bump me in the rear. I didn't know what to do."

Sheryl asked, "Harvey, what did you do?"

"I drove to a police station. I stopped and got out. When I saw the asshole leave, I just went inside and asked for directions. He was gone."

Keith said, "You did the right thing."

Ben finished with one more BenFree. "It's lucky for him because I was going to let the other shoe drop on him."

There was a silence followed by a collective sigh and sipping of drinks.

Sheryl asked, "Dan, haven't you had any experiences with violence?"

Dan looked into the distance and said "A few." He weighed whether to answer. "A long time ago, I was at a college party at this girl's house. Going great. It was crowded and the numbers were getting out of hand. And then these guys showed up and tried to crash. They were loud, overbearing, bullying. It was a town v. gown thing. No one wanted them there, but everyone was afraid to say anything. Then this fraternity kid tells them that they weren't invited. Pushing started. The lead crasher throws a punch and the frat guy blocks it, counters, and is clearly winning the fight. One of the other crashers shoves the guy from behind and distracts him. The next thing you know the first crasher knees him and he goes down. That was when it really began. This intruder kicked the other guy in the head. Hard. Over and over. I will never forget the sound—the horrible thud of the guy kicking the shit out of the other guy. He was bleeding, moaning and was going to be in need of medical attention."

Sheryl asked, 'What happened then?"

"That was when I learned an important lesson. Only the end result matters. There are no points for style in life. Fighting fair is fighting foolish."

Keith said, "You can say that again."

Larry said, "OK, fighting fair is fighting foolish." The brothers looked at each other and nodded; they had reached a tacit agreement. "We have a story that we both experienced." Keith nodded. "We both worked one summer in a resort. Keith was playing and singing, and I was waiting tables and doing odds and ends."

Keith chimed in, "They really were odd ends."

Larry began the story, "Anyway, there was this guy on the staff named Ryan. A real nice guy."

"A real big guy, too—a Golden Gloves boxer," commented Keith.

Larry was used to his brother interrupting. He continued, "Anyway (the word dragged out for effect), there was also a rent-a-cop. Picture Barney Fife, but heavy, mean and a little scary. He always wore this 'uniform'. Totally out of place at our resort."

Keith pointed out, "He was married to the owners' daughter. Everybody hated Fife-for-Life."

"So, anyway (the word had become a refrain), for some reason, they wanted to get rid of Ryan. They went around and got statements from the staff. When had we last seen him and what was he doing? We said we had seen him by the burger stand on the resort property eating a burger and drinking a coke."

"Then we found out he had been fired for drinking on the job," said Keith.

"It didn't make sense to any of us who knew him. Then we found out that they withheld his pay."

Larry said, "Anyway, at staff breakfast one morning, Ryan came in and quietly demanded his back pay from the owner."

"The owner ignored him."

"Anyway, they had words. It was getting tense."

"Then out of nowhere, the asshole cop jumps Ryan from behind and holds a .357 Magnum revolver to his head. Have you ever seen one of those hand cannons? Ryan could have squashed the Fife, but the cop Pearl Harbored him and cocked his pistol less than an inch from Ryan's head and starts screaming like an hysterical wild animal."

Keith said, "We've all seen people point and wave guns at each other in the movies and on TV. But this is a different thing. It was insane. We were sure that we were going to see a man die and maybe be covered in his brains ourselves."

"Anyway, they arrested him. Threw him in jail."

Keith said, "We went to be witnesses and found that they had forged our testimony to say that we had seen him drinking outside the burger stand."

"We couldn't find him. The cops just kept moving his location. The court docket kept changing. We never found out what happened to him."

The group was quiet for a moment and then they toasted their survival and turned to Dan. "This is getting depressing. How about some comic relief, Dan?" said Keith.

Dan responded, "OK, here's a riddle for the bright ones among you. What does an insomniac agnostic dyslexic do?""

The Devil's Jury knew that if the riddle was funny enough, it would serve as a "verdict" and the signal to adjourn. Individually, they shrugged.

Dan recited slowly, "An insomniac, agnostic dyslexic (dramatic pause) stays awake all night wondering if there really is a dog." One by one, they laughed as they got the joke.

The Jury began to adjourn. Some of the DJ members, including Larry and Sheryl, left the bar. Keith and Dan remained, drinking. Dan finished his drink, said good night and left. Keith waited about two minutes and followed. After discovering Dan's relationship with his brother's ex-wife, he decided to follow at a respectable distance to discover what other surprises there might be from Dan.

If Dan had an appointment or even a specific destination, it wasn't obvious to Keith. Daniels meandered, his pace fluctuating, his interest seeming to wander. Periodically he turned around and scanned the area. Keith reacted by hiding behind corners, in doorways. He stayed in the shadows. He wondered if Dan knew he was being followed or was just naturally suspicious. Stalking Dan was intriguing and adventurous. But as his quarry turned around for a protracted and intense look in his direction, Keith began to comprehend the reality of his situation. What would he do if he was discovered? If he discovered another rendezvous with Carolyn would he give in to his anger? Talk to him? Warn him? Slaughter the deceptive bastard who was hitting on his brother's ex-wife?

Daniels suddenly disappeared. Keith stopped and listened. After a moment, he heard footfalls fading away—which could only be Daniels at that hour. Darkness had banished the inhabitants of the area businesses.

He pursued the sound of his prey, unaware that they were passing the site of the notorious murder of the construction worker.

On a balcony overlooking the area, a bearded man was sneaking a cigarette, keeping the telltale tobacco odor out of his apartment. He was enjoying his smoke when two loud explosions ripped the air. He knew somehow that they were gunshots. Ducking instinctively, he eventually realized that the shots were too far away to be any danger to him. He waited, but heard no more. The bearded man returned to his apartment, decided that whatever it was, it was none of his business.

Divorce

"Divorce?" Kim shot out of her chair, almost spilling her coffee on the table.

Rob stifled a laugh and added as fast as he could, "Not us!!"

"Then who?"

"I want to discuss divorce in general. I mean, what do we really know about it?"

"Tell me Robert, what do we really know about marriage?"

Rob ventured, "Outside of our own, whose marriage do we know really well? And don't call me Robert, Kimberly."

"I really know only my own parents' marriage," Kim said. "And it was really extraordinary, possibly unique."

Rob asked the obvious, "My take on your parents' marriage is that it's a good one, probably one of the better ones that I'm aware of. Why was it unusual?"

"That's right; you probably don't know that my parents' marriage was arranged. In Korea when they were growing up, it was a common practice. You know that my older sister was born there, and by the time I was born two years later, my parents had moved from Seoul to northern California."

"I never would have guessed that your folks were in an arranged marriage. They seem so close."

"That's what makes their marriage so unusual. When I was little, the house was pretty formal. Quiet and non-demonstrative. Then when my sister and I became adolescents, everything changed."

"How?"

"It was like they discovered each other and fell in love."

Rob's eyes widened, "How did you know?"

Kim slapped her forehead, "My God, they were all over each other. My sister and I felt like we were the parents of very horny teenagers. We would tell them to get a room. And they would giggle and say that this was their room."

"I think it's kind of romantic," Rob said.

Kim smiled.

By now Kim was over the initial concern about their marriage and began to consider the ramifications of divorce, "Why are you so interested in divorce?"

"I have the feeling that the death of that lawyer is related to his being a divorce attorney. There seems to be a lot of animosity swirling around this guy and other people involved in divorces."

Kim thoughtfully put her hand to her chin, "You know, it's funny. A lot of real estate becomes available because of divorce. Some of the agents in our office even cultivate relationships with divorce attorneys. Hostility? I'm not sure what you'd call it, but I know that divorces are unhappy. Most people who go through it aren't big fans of their lawyers."

"I'm kind of used to divorcing spouses taking it out on each other. TRO's and spiteful or defensive actions.

"Hold on there, barrister, 'TRO'?"

"Temporary Restraining Order. To keep a toxic spouse or ex-spouse away and protect the subject and family from harm. Do you know how many exes threaten, maim or murder each other? In general, I think that's the more likely homicide suspect."

"You know I run into a lot of divorcees. Some are just happy to have a toxic person out of their lives."

Rob asked, "You've never really talked about your first marriage. What was that divorce like?"

Kim said, "Rob, we never really discussed it because it wasn't that important to me. It was one of those starter marriages. We were too young. Recklessly impulsive. It lasted less than a year. We weren't the people we were going to be."

"What happened to him?"

"I don't know. We stayed in touch for a few years, then lost track of each other."

Rob could see that the subject had been completed. "Interesting, but I'm trying to figure out what the motive would be for murder," Rob brought Kim back into focus.

"Isn't it usually money?"

"I don't see any profit motive in this case; might be personal."

"Don't some divorce attorneys make a lot of money? Don't they sometimes overcharge their clients?"

"Possibly, but I just interviewed a number of the victim's clients. Not much love, but not much hatred either."

"You'd think that a lawyer who had just crushed a former spouse for a lot of money would be beloved."

Rob mused, "You'd think..."

An idea visibly came to Kim. Her eyes widened. "What about the spouse who's just been crushed?

On the way to work the next morning, Rob reviewed the Monroe clients he had interviewed. He remembered that a couple were happy and got along well with their exes. It seemed unlikely that their former spouses would bear a grudge. A few who were living well had alluded to the fact their former mates had enough money to be generous to them. One or two had fared so poorly in their settlements that there was no chance that their exes would be upset with Carl Monroe. In fact, Rob had briefly considered them as suspects until their alibis or other reasons had ruled them out.

He decided that if he was going to re-interview any of the divorcees, he would do it in reverse order and start with Carolyn Johnston. Rob thought that it would make the most sense to interview her in a setting other than her home. Rather than meeting at his office, he felt that informal would be better. He called and arranged to have coffee with her at the end of her shift at the bakery/café. He realized that this meeting would likely be his final tactic in the investigation if he didn't gain new insights. He entered the shop at about 4:30 for his 5:00 meeting. He asked a woman wearing a jersey with shop's logo on it if Carolyn was available. As he waited, Carolyn came out from behind a curtain. She was also wearing the logo "Drinkin' Coffee" made in imitation of Dunkin' Donuts colors and fonts. He noted wryly to himself that Carolyn looked better in it than the woman who had greeted him.

"Hi Mr. Latrobe, I'll be with you in a minute."

"Call me Rob, how about if I sit at the table in the corner?"

Rob bought a coffee and decided to treat himself to pastry. Taking his coffee and carb to the table, he checked his smartphone while he waited. A few minutes later, Carolyn joined him with her own coffee. They exchanged pleasantries and discussed the reputation of the coffee shop, foot traffic, as well as other businesses in the area. Rob leaned forward, "Carolyn, I'm looking into new angles on the death of your former attorney."

Carolyn looked confused and possibly a little guilty to Rob.

Rob studied her carefully. He let his statement hang in the air. The silence grew to the point of being almost unbearable. Carolyn cleared her throat and mustered enough effort to look directly into Rob's eyes. "I didn't tell you everything. When I said that Monroe backed off when I warned him, it wasn't really accurate."

"You're talking about his advances toward you?"

"Yes, exactly. It wasn't once. He came on to me twice. I rejected him the first time and the second time I had to get very insistent. He called me names and threatened to tell Larry that he and I had made love."

"What happened?"

"I left. I made sure not to be alone with him. And it never came up again. I would have killed him myself if he tried again."

Rob waited before asking, "Carolyn, is that all?"

She held back tears, "Yes, that's all."

Rob went on, "I already explained that if the hit-and-run was not accidental or unavoidable, then it would seem that the only motive for such an act would be personal, some sort of vendetta. We've looked at his recent clients. It would have to be recent to be this combustible."

Carolyn nodded slowly.

He went on, "Can you give me a broader view of the emotions surrounding your divorce case? Who else is affected—the spouse, the opposing attorney, families, friends, children of the litigants, court personnel?"

Carolyn considered for a moment. She recalled the days of the divorce. Slowly she said, "Now that you mention it, my husband, his family and friends were very upset—enraged—his brother and some others, in particular. But I think that's to be expected. I was the one who wanted the divorce, and I think that Carl got me what I needed."

She took a sip of coffee; Rob seemed thoughtful as he took his. "Carolyn, I'd like you to think these next two questions over very carefully." He paused and looked at her intently. "Do you think that someone who thinks that they came out on the short end of a divorce case could react violently?"

Carolyn answered quickly and certainly, "Absolutely. You read about restraining orders and men killing or beating their exes all the…"

Rob cut in, "What about killing the attorney?"

"Well…."

Rob waited. Then he added, "Since this started, I've been informally interviewing friends and families of people going through divorce. You know what I've discovered? There's often a lot of bitterness to go around; it could even go viral—spread to friends and associates."

"Now that I think about it, Larry's family and friends were more hostile to Carl than they were to me."

She sat back, stared up at the white board specials without seeing them; her eyes blinked back a tear. "You know, Rob—I can call you Rob?—I really haven't thought about this in a long time. That was a scary time. I was overwhelmed by uncertainty, afraid of the fallout of the separation and divorce on my kids. I really only had contact with Keith, Larry's brother, and he was seething. He told me that the Gallon family was sure that the divorce went the way it did—so unfavorable and so bitterly contested—because of Carl Monroe."

Rob left wondering if the Gallons felt this way, how many other families might have hated Carl Monroe. The idea of him being the victim of someone's anger was becoming more likely than ever.

Pairing Up

The angry client angle was worth pursuing but there was one other avenue to travel to find the mysterious hit-and-run driver. Rob called Dizzy and they formulated a plan.

Later that afternoon just before closing time, Dizzy walked into the reception area of Reagan, Walker and Esposito. She had an appointment with Tom Reagan. The receptionist led her to a small meeting room where the lawyer waited.

He ushered Dizzy into a comfortable chair. "Good afternoon, Detective Gillespie. I don't think there's anything I can add to your investigation of the shooting, but I'd be glad to help."

His intercom alerted him to pick up his receiver. To Dizzy, "This must be important." Into the phone, "You know I'm in the middle of a meeting." He listened intently. His eyes widened for a moment and then he said, "Yes. Of course. Show him in."

Reagan looked puzzled. "Detective, I didn't know that the ADA was working on the shooting."

The door opened and Rob took a seat beside Dizzy. The secretary looked for further instructions and Reagan nodded her out the door.

Rob began with a brief preamble. "Mr. Reagan, we're here to offer you an opportunity." Dizzy watched Reagan's reactions and thought she detected stress.

"An opportunity? Are you selling me something?" Reagan tried humor to lighten the situation while he figured out what was going on.

Rob said, "Just how well did you know Carl Monroe?"

"I told you. We opposed each other in court on a number of occasions. Nothing more."

"So you never met outside of court?"

"I also told you that there may have been times we met to discuss cases. And that when we met in person the client was present."

Rob paused. Dizzy scribbled in her notebook as though she had just documented something important.

Reagan asserted himself. "What's this about?"

"Did you ever meet Mr. Monroe in the park?"

There was a one beat pause. "Yes. Maybe once or twice. Why?"

"Was there a client present?"

"I'm sure there was…."

Rob stared at the lawyer. Dizzy importantly wrote gibberish in her notebook. They waited. After an uncomfortable interval, Dizzy said, "can you give us the name of the client?"

Reagan shifted in his seat, exhaled deeply and quietly replied, "Me."

Now it was the investigators' turn to be puzzled. They looked at each other.

Rob said, "Please explain."

"All right, my wife had been talking about a divorce. So I went to Carl Monroe for counsel."

Dizzy said, "You went to the guy you despised?"

Reagan stood up, walked to the other side of the room and got a cup of coffee. He offered coffee to the others with a gesture. They were more interested in what he had to say. "It wasn't an easy decision emotionally, but it was by far the most pragmatic for at least three reasons."

Dizzy and Rob waited.

Reagan appeared to be summarizing for a jury. "First, if I retained Carl as my attorney, my wife couldn't. I had seen him turn too many divorces really ugly and spiteful really fast. I had to plan for the contingency that she would use Monroe to spite me. Second, I have so many occasions to interact with him that we could do it without arousing curiosity about my marital situation. Finally, I have a lot to lose and Carl really is good at winning the most for his clients."

After the meeting with Reagan, Rob and Dizzy walked over to the park where Reagan and Monroe had met. They watched a couple of kids playing "keep away" from a smaller kid. A senior couple sat on a bench taking turns throwing popcorn to a small flock of pigeons milling about like farm chickens.

Dizzy said, "I'll never understand treating pigeons like pets. They're like flying rats."

Rob said, "It's as close as you city folk get to wildlife." He was imitating the subtle drawl he had grown up with.

"No wildlife? Ever been to one of the titty bars on Route One?"

They sat and digested what they had just learned. Dizzy said, "I think that we can probably demote Reagan on the list of possibilities. Embarrassed but not murderous."

"I agree. So where does that leave us?"

"Well, we've tentatively eliminated one line of inquiry. And that's valuable."

"So I'll interview the rest of the clients and the more promising litigants. What about the Parker case?"

Dizzy said, "If your crime is intentional, it's personal and Monroe's profession and style could yield a bunch of suspects with no payoff. With Jack Parker it's likely anything but personal and so far not a single suspect or a motive."

Rob said, "You know, I've been thinking about it. We seem to be heading toward thinking that Parker was killed by a stranger."

"True. Because there's no real motive. Even the neighbors who oppose the construction gain nothing from his death. It wouldn't make sense for them to commit the crime."

"Of course not. The show must go on. Maybe we're looking too hard for a motive, a benefit."

Dizzy said, "That's a good point, with Monroe we're hypothesizing revenge. Totally emotional."

They said almost in unison, "There is no rational motive."

Dizzy said, "We couldn't figure out who would want to kill Jack Parker."

"Or who would benefit."

Dizzy said, "No one does."

Rob said, "You've investigated more felonies than I have; I have no idea where to look."

"My dad used to say that sometimes you have to wait for the solution to come to you."

They agreed to brainstorm on their own and join forces after Rob finished his interviews or in the unlikely event that a piece would fall into place.

Disappearance

It was Wednesday night, commonly a night for the Devil's Jury to meet at Bar None. Larry and Sheryl and three others ordered drinks and waited for Keith and Dan. It was possible that Keith was working in the back and Dan could be anywhere, waiting to make a grand entrance. Without Dan, its de facto master of ceremonies, the group was quieter—fewer laughs. In the absence of Dan's empirical and technological knowledge, they often complained about the miseries of technology in the full glory of their ignorance—useless passwords, malicious hackers, as well as unnecessary and harmful updates. After they finished complaining about Apple, Microsoft, and Google, they decided to call it a night. Neither Dan nor Keith appeared.

When the DJ convened several nights later, Keith was there; Dan was not. Keith asked where Dan was and acted surprised when he was told that he hadn't been seen for several days. Drinks were ordered, appetizers delivered, and the group carried on as it always did. Throughout the evening, Keith was quieter than usual; he seemed distracted and concerned.

For several days, Sheryl and the others tried to contact Dan or find his whereabouts through whatever means they could—at his apartment and through the IT firms he contracted with. They tried his health club and other bars he was known to frequent. Larry even called Dan's sister in the Midwest. After four days, Larry declared Dan a missing person.

At the police station they filed a report with the names of Dan's frequent contacts and places he visited. In addition, they posted several photographs of him on the bulletin board, in the hope that someone might recognize him now or from the past. Dizzy remembered that handsome face from her investigation of the public works worker, and she had a vague feeling that she had seen him more than once.

A search of Dan's place offered no clues. There was no evidence of abduction or flight. During the search, they uncovered pay stubs from several of his IT jobs as well as a couple of shot glasses from Bar None. It was the glass with the slogan *The Best Bar—Bar None* that triggered Dizzy's memory of seeing him the night she went for drinks with her colleague.

Dizzy thought Bar None was worth a second visit. After all, Dan's group was not far from the shooting or the hit-and-run. She entered Bar None and inquired about Dan and the group she had seen. Nielsen told her that the group would probably be in later. He mentioned that a member of the group tended bar there—Keith Gallon. To find out more about Dan's disappearance, Dizzy arranged to meet with the group one person at a time as they came in. Nielsen made a small back room storage area available for the interviews. Meetings with Larry and Sheryl and a couple of others allowed Dizzy to conjure up a picture of Dan as a convivial and charming person of possibly questionable morals and definitely questionable judgment. No one could think of any enemies Dan might have or any reason for him to take off. When Keith showed up for work he was encouraged by the manager to speak to the detective.

After a few preliminary questions from Dizzy, Keith slumped in the chair and stared into the distance. He said, "I don't know where he is. A few nights ago, I followed him. I had found out that he was seeing my brother's ex-wife. I started to wonder what else he was up to, what other secrets he might have. I was right behind him, and he disappeared in the shadows."

Dizzy looked Keith in the eyes.

"I think he fired two shots at me. I know it sounds unbelievable, but they were definitely gunshots. Fired by Dan at me."

"What did you do?"

"I ducked and hugged the ground. I waited. Then I heard the scuffle of running feet. After three minutes that seemed like twenty, I ran back in the direction I had come from. I scrambled and stumbled through dark streets, totally gripped by panic. I stopped and leaned against a building to catch my breath in a well-lit area. With people exiting or smoking outside restaurants and bars, I felt safer there. I had no idea what I should do. Should I tell someone? The police? What if those weren't gunshots I heard? I hadn't <u>seen</u> anything. I turned into the nearest bar, ordered a Jack Daniel's before I realized how ironic that was—Dan always ordered Jack Daniel's. I drained the shot and left for home—having no idea what to do."

Dizzy looked intently at Keith, "Why didn't you report the shots?"

"When I didn't hear anything about shots being fired, I began to doubt that they were real shots. I decided to wait and see how Dan acted, what he said."

"Weren't you a little afraid? He might try to kill you again…"

"I stayed at home trying to process what was going on for a couple of days."

"Then?"

"I couldn't stay there forever. I had to find out what was going on."

"You didn't tell anyone? Not your brother, a friend?" Then Dizzy added, "A priest?"

Keith shook his head, "I didn't want to look foolish."

Dizzy paused long enough to make Keith uncomfortable, "How about looking guilty?"

Keith reacted with intensity for the first time, "Guilty of WHAT?"

"Think about it, Daniels has been reported as a Missing Person. He is, or was, your friend. Not only don't you appear to be worried about him, but you also admit to being the last person to see him. Alive, anyway."

Keith looked pale, "Oh, my God!!"

Dizzy pushed on, "How did you find out that he was seeing your brother's ex-wife, Carolyn is it?"

"I think I'd better call an attorney."

"Maybe you should…. And I hate to sound like an old TV detective, but don't leave town."

———— ꝏ꙾ꙮꝏꙮꝏ ————

Kim ran for the phone, expecting that Rob would be late as usual. It was Rob, but he surprised her, "Hi, honey, it's yaw lovah. Ah'll be home shortly. Prepauh yourself dahlin, I mean to have my way with you." She was surprised and delighted. Usually after a day of work he forgot such niceties as love and marriage. She paused and drawled in her best Scarlett O' Hara, "Why suh, whatever do you mean?"

When he arrived at home forty five minutes later, Kim greeted him in tight jeans and heels. Nothing else. And nothing else excited him as much. After kissing and fondling, she led him into the bedroom. She walked over to the bedroom lamp, slowly and purposely leaned over, dangling her ample breasts in the brilliant light. She looked at him, winked and then drawled melodramatically, "I can't stand a naked light bulb," in her best Blanche Dubois. Then she shut off the light. After they made love, they hugged for almost twenty minutes. Then they sat silently at the kitchen table and ate chicken sandwiches and tomato salads and drank beer.

Rob decided not to reveal Reagan's marital issues. Better kept private. He recounted his visit to the bakery and his possible new approach to the Monroe case.

Kim said, "So if I follow your thinking, you are going to widen your search to all the people who may have been pissed off recently at the attorney, client or adversary."

"At this point, we're looking more closely at adversaries. Process of elimination." Rob got up and paced. "So far none of his own clients seem likely."

"What about friends, relatives or girlfriends?"

"None that we're aware of."

"What about past clients, not recent?"

Rob said, "We may get there eventually, but the heat and anger of the hit-and-run indicate intense feelings that couldn't be suppressed for very long."

"So?"

"One whole family was violently upset by the way they were treated. But that's not the most important reason to examine them."

"OK, Sherlock, what's the most important reason?"

"We don't have any other promising direction."

"Does this detective—Gillespie—agree?"

"Yes. And you can call her 'Dizzy'."

"So Dizzy agrees."

"Yes. And there is one other possibility."

"What's that?"

"It's just an accidental hit-and-run."

———— ⁓⁓⁓⁓⁓⁓ ————

A few days later, Rob interviewed the members of the Gallon family. He began with those identified by Carolyn as Larry's most ardent supporters, most hostile toward Carl Monroe. She excluded his parents from the list of possible interviewees because they had moved to their retirement home in the Midwest. A contributing factor was their despondency over the divorce and their sadness over the loss of Carolyn as a daughter-in-law.

Larry's brother Keith, his friends Dan and Sheryl and, of course, Larry were at the top of the list. Rob decided to take Carolyn's suggestion and reach them and Larry at Bar None, just down the street.

Rob arrived a little after 3:00 and asked for the owner. He handed over his card and while he waited, he looked around the bar. The walls were covered with photographs of athletic teams from nearby schools interspersed with logos of beers and photos of colorful peppers and hot chicken wings. In the middle of the photos, there were a couple of college diplomas bearing the name Michael Nielsen. There were some class photos of graduation with a man who Rob assumed was Mr. Nielsen.

Even as a young man, Nielsen looked professorial. On the wall to the right of the bar were several diplomas and certificates. Rob wandered over and scanned them. There was a real estate license, a photo of the same man on a nice boat, and a photo of him in a tuxedo holding a trophy with a dancing couple on it. Several minutes later, a man in a white shirt emerged from the back, definitely older, grayer, balding, and heavier, but also definitely Michael Nielsen.

To put him at ease, Rob asked him about the photos. Nielsen cleared his throat and as he began to answer, Rob thought to himself, "He's about to deliver a lecture."

"I have a varied history. I've sold real estate, worked as a locksmith, I have a boat and I have competed in ballroom dancing around the world. Did most of them at the same time."

"That's pretty impressive. You're a multi-faceted guy."

Feeling that his credentials had been established, Nielsen took some interest in his interrogating guest and asked, "How about you, Mr. Latrobe. Are you involved in any endeavors beyond criminal law?"

Rob leaned on the bar, "Call me Rob, Mr. Nielsen." Wanting to appear as well-versed as his acquaintance, Rob said, "I spend as much free time as possible playing jazz piano."

"Call me Michael. Ever do any gigs?"

"Occasionally."

Nielsen pointed to a piano in a corner, "Maybe you can play here someday. What kind of jazz do you play? Who are your heroes?"

Rob said, "The usual—mostly bop and post-bop mainstream. On piano, I like everyone from Oscar and Bill Evans to Keezer and Ozone; there are a lot of good ones."

Nielsen shook his head in understanding.

Rob then explained his task and asked about the group.

"We have several groups who meet informally; this bar is built on its reputation as a local tavern. Our patrons are mostly frequent social imbibers who congregate here for communal amusement."

"What about the bunch that your bartender is part of?"

"You mean the group of which my bartender is a member," Nielsen corrected.

Rob nodded.

"Those who are friends with my bartender?"

Rob thought to himself "what a pompous ass" and smiled and nodded.

"Keith works for me. Keith Gallon." Nielsen smiled, "His associates make up a fine group. Convivial. Drink a lot. Talk a lot. Laugh a lot."

"I'd like to talk to them—and him."

"I can comply with your former request but not the latter. That crowd is likely to arrive shortly."

Rob asked, "And Keith?"

"Mr. Latrobe, I'm afraid that it looks like Keith is in a bit of trouble. A female police detective interviewed members of the group about a missing comrade."

"Missing comrade?"

"That Irish fellow who's always drinking American whiskey has apparently gone missing."

"Why do you think Keith is in trouble?"

"As soon as the detective interviewed him, he took off as though he were on fire... and he did not look happy."

"You said it was a female detective, do you remember the detective's name?"

"She was an attractive black woman, very professional."

Rob decided to forego the other interviews. He figured that the detective was Dizzy and he would call her as soon as he left the bar. He wondered about Dizzy's interest in Keith. Maybe their cases would intersect. "What can you tell me about Keith Gallon? How long has he tended bar for you?'

"He's been with me for a while. We were mates, drinking buddies, oddly enough."

"Oddly enough?"

"Yes, it's odd because I gave up drinking."

Rob thought there was more to the story so he remained silent.

Nielsen slowly passed his palm over his bald head, "Suffice it to say that in my time I saw enough of alkies cheating each other or prevaricating to their friends to make me want to stay sober and on my guard. I found that when I was drinking I'd get violently angry—especially with people who lied."

Rob filed that information in the Not Quite Suspects folder in his mind and brought the conversation back on track, "So how good a bartender is Keith?"

"To tell you the truth, he's average." Nielsen paused, "Truthfully as a mixologist he is a real wanker—a below average bartender." Rob shrugged his shoulders in an inquiring gesture.

Nielsen clarified, "Keith doesn't pour precisely. He can be overly generous. I probably lose profit on some of his drinks. What makes it worse is that he can be slow."

Rob pinched his lower lip and mused. Finally he asked the obvious "Why do you keep him here?"

Nielsen exhaled and answered, "Keith definitely has other talents. In fact I met him through music. He and that Irish-American fellow, Dan Daniels, used to play a bit. Guitars and singing. Mostly funny songs or little known ditties. I played a little banjo and mandolin and would jam with them from time to time." Rob noted not for the first time the crispness of Nielsen's t's in *time to time*. Nielsen continued, "I found out that he was easy to be with, talk to, and even to work with. He's the social bloke who makes the tavern work. He's well-liked and he's great at connecting people up and putting them at ease. I think he's a major reason many of our regulars are regulars. And they probably don't notice that his drinks can be inconsistent or slowly produced."

Rob tried for more background information. "Mr. Nielsen, what can you tell me that's unusual or revealing about the others? In particular, the missing guy."

Nielsen cleared his throat, "Dan Daniels." Rob wrote in his notebook.

Nielsen continued, warming up to his subject. "It's a funny thing. If I think back far enough, Dan and Keith came together, almost as a package. They arrived at about the same time. Sang together."

"And?"

Nielsen shrugged in a "who knows?" response and poured himself a glass of ginger ale, most likely to keep himself distracted while alcohol was being consumed. Rob filed that away as well. He thanked Mr. Nielsen and left to contact Dizzy.

The Fugitive

"Hi Detective Gillespie," Rob greeted Dizzy when she answered her direct line.

"That's 'Dizzy' to you, or even 'Diz', Rob," she smiled to herself at the sound of a friendly voice. "To what do I owe the pleasure?"

Rob decided to get right to it. "What's the story with Keith Gallon?"

"I'm afraid that's going to cost you—if not a drink, at least a cup of coffee."

Rob certainly didn't mind the idea of coffee, but was surprised by the lack of a direct, short answer. He dramatized the effort of compliance and slowly replied in an exaggerated aw shucks way, "Well, I suppose I could, maybe, that is, I think…"

Dizzy cut off his act, "Seriously, Rob, the answer to that question is complicated and isn't fully formed yet; it might be helpful to examine the situation together." Dizzy thought that finding Dan Daniels was becoming urgent because she felt it was tied to her case in some way. Besides, relief from the tedium of the office was appealing. "How about coffee?"

"Sounds fine."

"How about now?"

A half hour later they met in a sandwich shop and ordered two coffees. Dizzy opened with, "How can you possibly be looking at the guy in my case? Did you give up on the hit-and-run?"

"Not at all, that's why I want to interview Keith Gallon, but it's a real long shot," Rob responded.

Dizzy's eyes sparkled with bemused humor.

Rob added, "A super, gigantic, way-out-on-a-limb shot."

"I'm listenin', how could this guy tie in to your case?"

"Well, I am convinced that this hit-and-run is really a 'drive-over-and-murder' case and I decided to interview people who might resent Mr. Monroe to see if anyone in that situation might be prone to violence…"

"My God, Rob, you are either really tenacious or you don't have enough work."

"Well, it could be my last shot. After this I'm temporarily closing the file on this. Now what is it about my talking to Keith Gallon that is so complicated?"

Dizzy shifted in her seat and exhaled. She related how Dan Daniels was missing; his clothes and possessions were intact; none of his friends had been notified. The last one to see him alive was Keith Gallon. Gallon had admitted to following Daniels with no credible motive. "So the long and short of it is that since I haven't charged him yet, I don't know where he fits in this. But I am interested in talking to him, even if he is lawyered up. I would be fascinated to see what he has to say about your case."

They set off together to find Keith. They started back at the bar, figuring that Keith might show up to work or if he didn't, his friends might be there and know where he was. Mike Nielsen was working behind the bar, setting up for the evening's business. He looked a little surprised to see Dizzy and Rob together, "I haven't seen Mr. Gallon since you two were here to inquire about him. What has he done? Have you found that Daniels chap yet? I hope he's okay."

"We hope so too," Dizzy said. "Do you expect any of them here tonight?"

"I would anticipate the group will make its appearance later; I can only hope that Keith and Dan will be among them. Or they'll know where to find them."

Julie Harvey heard her doorbell and looked out the window. There was a mail truck idling at the curb. She went to the door and accepted a box from the mailman. It was a cardboard box a little bigger than a shoe box. The letter taped to the outside was from The Patient. She slowly opened the envelope, unfolded and read the letter:

Ms. Harvey,

This is the box I asked you about in our last session. Please keep it unopened as you promised. If I don't come in person to pick it up by the end of the month, please open it and do what you think is right with the contents. It is comforting to know that you are one person I can trust.

Julie read The Patient's signature. She circled the first day of the next month in red on her calendar.

Keith knew he was in a pickle. Things were happening to him at the speed of light. Most of the shocks to his system emanated from Dan Daniels. First he witnesses Daniels with his brother's ex-wife, then Daniels leads him into an apparent trap, next Daniels shoots a gun at him to scare him or maybe even kill him, and finally Daniels disappears—all leaving Keith under suspicion of causing Dan's absence with no way to prove his innocence.

He thought of calling an attorney, but prior to that he had to find someone who knew his situation, his environment. Maybe his brother, but Keith didn't want to have to reveal that he had discovered Daniels with Carolyn. How would he explain not telling Larry? What reason could he give for following Daniels? He really didn't know why he did it. Would Larry suspect that Keith had somehow done away with Daniels?

For the time being anyway. The only remaining course was Sheryl.

Rob and Dizzy left the bar, planning to return when and if the group reconvened. Dizzy wanted to search for Dan, and Rob was feeling that something was up with this group of people. They decided to team up to search for Dan and/or Keith. They were concerned that they might freak members of the group if the two of them showed at the bar together. So they adjourned to the coffee shop down the block where Carolyn Johnston (Gallon) worked to see if they could work it through to gain more insight into the situation.

Rob and Dizzy entered the coffee shop and were immediately greeted by Carolyn with a familiar smile for Rob and a quizzical look for Dizzy. They sat in a corner. Carolyn came right over with two cups and a pot of coffee. Rob introduced Dizzy as Detective Gillespie in charge of investigating the disappearance of Dan Daniels.

Carolyn turned white as an over-bleached sheet, actually swayed a bit, held onto a chair at the table and sat down.

Rob half stood over her, put his hand on her shoulder and asked, "Are you all right?"

Carolyn gained her composure and apologized, "It's just that I had no idea.... How long has it been since he's been 'missing'?"

Dizzy replied, "At least a week."

"Maybe he's just on a trip."

"No signs of preparation. His luggage is still there, he didn't tell anyone—not his friends or the people who regularly contract him out for IT work." They paused while Carolyn apparently processed the information. "Carolyn, if you don't mind my asking...."

When some of Carolyn's co-workers looked inquisitive, Dizzy gave them a reassuring gaze that said the situation was under control. Carolyn knew where the question was heading and her eyes began to glisten with tears, "Dan and I had a special relationship; we became closer in the last couple of months. I guess the word would be 'intimate'.

Rob asked, "Did anyone know about this?"

"Are you kidding? Larry and Keith would probably be bullshit. Maybe others ...." The waitress slowly shook her head from side to side.

"What can you tell us to help us find him?" Dizzy didn't offer any of her suspicions of foul play.

"I can't think of anything right now; I'm really too upset. Maybe later."

Dizzy left her card, and as they departed, Carolyn told them that Keith, Larry, and Sheryl were likely to have more to offer.'

———⟶∾∾⟵———

Sheryl was leaving her office, and practically bumped into Keith. He pulled her aside, said he had been looking for her. "You've been looking for me?" She stopped him and looked into his eyes. "Keith, how are you? I'm concerned. Dan is missing. I understand that the police are about to arrest you. What do you know about it? What's going on?"

They started walking together. "I honestly don't know. I have no idea where Dan is. I wish I knew. I think he may have even taken shots at me."

"Shots? What are you talking about?"

Keith told her the story he had told the police.

"Oh, Keith, that's terrifying. How did the cops react?"

Keith held Sheryl's shoulders and gazed deeply into her eyes. "Then you believe me?"

She stared back, "It's really an incredible, extraordinary story. But yes, I believe you. I believe you because I believe in you."

"Thanks, I really need that. I don't have anybody else to turn to."

"What about Larry?"

"I thought about it. But… if I told him, I'd have to tell him about Carolyn and Dan."

"I don't understand."

"I just wouldn't know how. How would I explain that I never told him? I just can't face it. Along with everything else that seems to be happening."

Sheryl asked, "How can I help? What's your next step?"

"I think I have to disappear for a while. I have to figure this out. In the meantime, you didn't see me, we didn't talk. You could get in trouble. Don't mention anything—especially about Dan and Carolyn, and Dan and me."

They hugged—each hoping it wasn't the last time.

———ᴡᴠᴏᴏᴇᴛᴏᴏᴛᴇᴏᴏᴡᴡ———

Rob and Dizzy re-entered the bar and were greeted by, "Ah, my new regulars, the constabulary," Nielsen nodded toward a table in the corner. As they worked their way over to the table, Rob wondered if the salutation had been a discreet warning to the group.

Dizzy approached the table ahead of Rob. There were only four people around the table as the evening was young. Dizzy handed out business cards and introduced herself and Rob as her 'associate,' "We're looking for Dan Daniels and Keith Gallon—or information leading to them. What are your names?"

One of the young men stood up almost ceremoniously, "This is Sheryl Common, Ben Freeman, and Sally Intrilligator. I'm Larry Gallon, Keith's brother and Dan's friend." Larry sat down and leaned back.

Rob stepped forward, "Do you know where your brother is?"

The others looked to Larry who replied, "If I knew, I'd be talking to him now. And if I knew where Dan was, I'd kick his ass for getting us all worried."

The others nodded assent. The tall, bald one looked stricken by the situation.

Dizzy asked, "Do you have any ideas where we might start?"

They looked at each other and Sheryl said, "Larry and I are the ones who know them best, and we have no idea where to start."

"Have you been to Keith's or Dan's apartments?"

"No, how would we get in? They don't answer their phones; we've emailed, and knocked," said Sheryl with Larry nodding.

Dizzy looked at them intently, "We can get you in, would you like to come with us? Your perspective could be helpful."

Larry and Sheryl looked at each other, nodded, slid back their chairs and stood. They gave small waves to their compatriots and said they'd see them the following night.

Rob and Dizzy led Sheryl and Larry to Dizzy's car. Rob sat in the back with Larry; Sheryl sat in the passenger seat. Sheryl directed Dizzy to Dan's place; Dizzy didn't mention that she had been there already. It was a short ride, and the investigators restricted their conversation to small talk. It would help them to relax, build some trust, and provide a baseline of their attitudes and demeanor, possibly an insight into their truthfulness.

They pulled up to the address and got out together. They opened the door and found the apartment as Dizzy had last seen it—relatively neat, with the usual single male affronts to cleanliness. There were some dirty clothes strewn about here and there, open books, towels that had dried on the bathroom floor. There were no indications that he had planned to go anywhere, a fact underscored by the suitcase in the closet.

After they had glanced around the premises, Dizzy turned to Larry and Sheryl, "Any ideas? If he went anywhere, where would he go?"

"I have no idea," said Sheryl.

Larry looked thoughtful, "He sometimes went hiking. We all do."

Dizzy noted, "I don't see any boots or a backpack."

Larry said, "That could mean that he went hiking, or...."

Rob repeated, "Or?"

"There was a shed out back that he shared with a couple of other units. I think that he kept all his outdoor gear there" Sheryl noted.

After showing ID, they procured a key from a neighbor. The group went outside and opened the door. They found Dan.

Dan's Place

Dan wasn't in good shape. In fact he was very dead. Sheryl and Larry stared for a moment and then bailed. Outside the shed, Rob stayed close as Sheryl sobbed and Larry looked as though he might vomit. Dizzy remained inside and called the coroner. The lack of blood or signs of struggle suggested that the crime had not taken place in the shed. They followed procedure and cordoned off the area. There were two gunshot wounds, one in the shoulder and the fatal shot in the neck. The latter wound would have excreted large amounts of blood. Dizzy was thankful that she didn't have to deal with blood or spatter. Tests would reveal if copious amounts of blood had been bleached out at the scene. Dizzy was certain that Dan had been shot elsewhere and moved there. Hell, there was barely room for the body itself in the crowded space.

A short time later, Doc McCann confirmed Dizzy's suspicions. She left him to his tasks and knew that the team investigating the scene was unlikely to turn up anything significant. Seeing how upset Larry and Sheryl were and feeling exhausted themselves, Rob and Dizzy agreed to meet Dan's two mourning friends the next day at the police station so they could talk without distractions.

Larry and Sheryl arrived together the next day and were ushered into an interrogation room. They looked awful. Apparently, they had gone to their respective homes to escape and sleep. It had required almost an hour of consoling each other by phone and text as well as several sleeping pills.

They settled in the room, briefly holding hands for mutual support and comfort. Dizzy joined them. Noting that Rob was going to join them soon, she did what she could to put them at ease. When Rob arrived, he could see by their body language and Sheryl's red eyes and pallor that they were both still upset by Dan's death.

Dizzy addressed the two friends, "We really appreciate your coming here and we're sorry for your loss. We're hoping that the four of us can figure out how to bring Dan's killer to justice."

Larry said, "We're here to help…if we can."

Dizzy added, "Finding Keith could be the key."

"We don't want to drag you back to the unpleasantness of the shed…." Dizzy opened a laptop, tapped a key and swung it around to face them, "You'll recognize that this is a video of the interior of the shed. The body has been removed."

Upon hearing the word "body," Sheryl began to sob. Larry put his arm around her.

Dizzy continued, "You can use the cursor to focus on any part of the room and you can click on the icon to zoom in. We want to know if anything is out of place or gives any clue as to what happened."

They turned their attention to the screen. The camera surveyed the room slowly. They showed little or no reaction. Rob grunted a muted comment and leaned against the wall behind Larry and Sheryl. Arms folded, he looked as though he didn't want to be there. Dizzy studied the two witnesses while they studied the screen. Periodically she prodded them. "Does that look familiar? Is anything out of place?"

As Larry and Sheryl focused on the monitor, Rob moved to stand over their shoulders. He spoke for the first time and asked of no one in particular, "What's the point of inspecting the shed? Don't we all know that Keith is the key to this?"

He turned Larry's chair to face him. "His brother and his best friend, and you can't tell us where he is? We want to help him." He crowded Larry, invading his space. Softly but threateningly, Rob clearly demanded, "Where the hell is your brother? He did this, didn't he? Where is he? Now!!"

Sheryl held herself and wept. Larry looked at Dizzy. Finding no relief there, he gathered himself and looked Rob in the eye. His response reflected his own frustration, "I have no idea. I wish I did."

Rob looked disgusted and turned abruptly and left the room. Larry put his arm around Sheryl, looked pleadingly at Dizzy and said, "What's his problem? We've lost a close friend and I'm worried as hell about my brother."

"Let's calm down, you two are the most likely people to help us find Keith and resolve this situation. Look at the 360° of the shed, what should it tell us about Dan's murder? Is anything missing? What did he use the shed for?"

Larry sat back, crossed his arms and said, "It was kind of a staging area for his outdoor activities. You can see his skis, a tent, and a couple of backpacks."

Sheryl added, "You know, some of us kind of shared his stuff; he always had several backpacks, hiking poles, insulated clothes. He was like a walking L. L. Bean."

Larry noted, "It looks like one of the backpacks might be missing." He turned to Sheryl, "I remember. It was Keith's favorite—the forest green one."

Sheryl just nodded. Dizzy could see that they were tiring. She thought it would be best to conclude with that positive discovery. "Thank you for your help, please keep thinking and call me if you have any ideas."

Larry and Sheryl nodded and left.

Dizzy watched them leave and then Rob re-entered. He had been watching through the one way window. Dizzy said, "Wow, watched a lot of Law and Order, have you? You really know how to play Bad Cop."

"Well, we wanted to wake them up and get an unguarded reaction," Rob noted defensively alluding to their plan. "We both think that they're holding something back. So... Detective, did you detect anything?"

"Not yet. But there's something there," Dizzy answered. "What happened to Keith?"

Just then Dizzy's phone rang. She answered it, gave Rob a look of recognition. What followed was a lot of thoughtful eye movement and 'okays' ending with Dizzy agreeing to meet the caller the following day at 11:00.

Dizzy arrived at 10:50 and watched the rain streak down the picture window of the coffee shop while she waited for Sheryl. Carolyn was not working that shift, which was just as well. She hoped that Sheryl hadn't gotten cold feet.

Sheryl showed up at 11:00 sharp. She looked anxious, "I wanted to meet you alone. I don't think I like Mr. Latrobe," she paused, "and I don't feel good about what I'm going to tell you."

Dizzy waited.

"It's what Keith told me, and I promised not to tell anyone."

Gillespie said quietly, "If you think it's going to help…."

"Keith said he was going to have to disappear for a while, try to figure out the situation."

"Did he tell anyone else?"

"I don't think so. That's why I don't feel good about telling you. He trusted me." She leaned forward, hiding her face. Dizzy waited. After a long two minutes, Sheryl raised her head and looked pleadingly at the detective, "But I don't know who else is in a position to help."

"What about Larry?"

"I don't think he can do anything, and if Keith was going to tell him, he would have told me. Larry's his brother and they were close, but Keith and I have a special relationship."

Dizzy smiled.

"Not that kind of relationship. We just spend a lot of time together and tell each other everything."

Sheryl played with the muffin she had ordered while Dizzy sipped.

"Sheryl, let's think about this. Where would Keith go to disappear?"

Sheryl shook her head slowly from side to side.

"Where does he go to be alone? Was there anywhere you and he went that might fit the description?"

Sheryl raised her eyes to meet Dizzy's, "What will you do if you find him?"

"He has a lot of questions to answer and can help a lot of people who are concerned about him. He may not know Dan's dead. He may have been afraid of whoever killed Dan. And, of course, he may have had something to do with it. But I don't intend to hurt him...I might not even arrest him."

Sheryl hesitated, thought.

"Sheryl, he needs our help."

"I've been thinking about places where Keith might feel safe, not be discovered. He and I kind of thought of it as a refuge. It's the White Mountains."

Dizzy waited patiently.

"Keith and I used to talk about places to retreat to. There are a few. But if he's hiding it would be in a more remote inaccessible place than he and I ever went to together."

Dizzy was intrigued. "Who else would know what those places were? Larry?"

"Larry probably knows those places better than I do."

"I don't have a problem if Larry wants to help. The more, the merrier."

"Larry's not sure he wants to find Keith. I think he feels a little guilty. He's not sure he wants to know what happened."

"Can you talk to him? It's really best for Keith and everybody."

Sheryl said, "I'll try my best. If I can get him to go, it's a few hours' ride from here."

Dizzy looked intently into the concerned woman's eyes, "Sheryl, I'm counting on you. It sounds like we should go first thing in the morning. With or without Larry."

Headin' North

Early the next morning Dizzy picked up Sheryl at her house. She was encouraged to see Larry there.

Dizzy took a look at the pair as they deposited their gear in her trunk. They were dressed for hiking. Each wore several layers on top—t-shirt, shirt, vest and jacket. In the trunk of the car each had a backpack and hiking boots. Sheryl carried a walking stick and they both looked comfortable and prepared for their destination. Their attire showed signs of considerable wear. Dizzy, on other hand, looked uncomfortable, like she had just left the store with most of the hiking gear they had for sale.

Larry asked, "Hike much?" while Sheryl smiled.

Dizzy smiled, "I've seen *Jeremiah Johnson* and *A Walk in the Woods*, isn't that enough?"

The sun was shining and as they headed north, Dizzy hoped that the time wouldn't be wasted and that they would find Keith or clues to his whereabouts. One way or another, Keith could be the key to solving Dan's death.

Dizzy drove quietly and watched the road, allowing Larry and Sheryl to relax. She avoided any resemblance to an inquiry or interrogation. She kind of floated above and listened as much as she could while Larry and Sheryl chatted, possibly trying to relax each other.

They had been traveling for over two hours. Dizzy had the persistent feeling that either Larry or Sheryl or both knew more than they were saying. It was even more likely than that they hadn't discovered or faced some critical clue. What was going on with Keith or who had killed Dan had to be in front of them in some way. Sort of like searching a room several times for your car keys totally without success. When you find them, it finally dawns on you that you really knew where they were all along.

Rather than trying to pull the information out of her passengers, Dizzy thought the best way for the secret to come to the surface was for them to continue their conversation. Almost forget that she was there. She heard Larry ask Sheryl, "Who could have killed Dan? Do you think it's someone we know?" Dizzy watched the approaching mountains and listened to the sound of the road under the tires.

Sheryl replied slowly, "I suppose it would have to be, but who do we know that could be a murderer. Really evil?"

Larry said, "I've been thinking about it, and I really can't picture anyone we know as being a real criminal."

Sheryl closed her eyes to concentrate and said, "You know sometimes when I watch the news and there's been a murder, I notice that a lot of the times, it starts with the neighbors talking about how the killer was a nice, quiet guy. Then after a couple of days, they're talking about how the guy was always crazy or mean or criminal."

"In other words, the act defines the guy, not the other way around."

"Right, we all think that people who kill others are a different breed," Sheryl said.

Dizzy couldn't resist joining in the conversation, "Statistically a lot of them are. A staggering number of murders are committed by habitual, deep down criminals, usually psychopaths or sociopaths."

Larry asked, "What about the guy who kills his lover or a friend, unpremeditated?"

Sheryl added, "I was thinking that there are times when you come close to violence and maybe you just impulsively do the wrong thing. Does that mean that you've been a bad person all your life?"

Dizzy said, "We're going to stop at the next information booth so I can make contact with the New Hampshire State Police as a courtesy. They might join us or at least tell me about where we're headed. Or maybe more important, where we are."

Sheryl said, "I've been hiking with Keith and Larry, Dan has gone fishing with a couple of the others…. Anyway, it popped into my head that on those hikes we sometimes fantasized that the trails in the White Mountains would be a great place to get away. *To get lost.*"

Larry nodded, "These mountains cover a huge area. Even though we've been all over them, it would be like finding a specific needle among stacks of needles. Fortunately, Keith had his favorite places and we know most of them."

Sheryl added, "And there are only a few places we hike a lot that are out of the way enough for Keith to expect he wouldn't see any other tree-huggers or hikers. He'd be left alone."

Larry shook his head in agreement, "We should definitely look for the most isolated trails."

After a while, the trio decided to make a pit stop. Detective Gillespie said, "The police department will be happy to buy you lunch for your help and I'll call into the state police." They stopped at a small general store that offered a variety of outdoors accessories. Dizzy made a call hoping for support from the state police, but was told that a huge accident was requiring all their manpower. They were on their own. They stopped to pick up sandwiches for the trail at a small general store choosing to ignore the fact that the place also sold live bait,. As they left the parking lot, a dark blue car followed them.

An hour and a half later, Sheryl and Larry started discussing in low tones which area was the most likely place to find Keith. Then Sheryl reported out to Dizzy, "The most isolated place we know that Keith has been to is "Owl's Head." Several miles later they directed Dizzy to a trailhead parking lot. Dizzy thought it certainly was remote and isolated, several turns and a couple of miles down a bumpy, mostly untraveled road that was more like a car-wide path. At the end, there was a gravel parking lot. It had a capacity for about a half dozen cars. There was one there—a black SUV. Sheryl and Larry looked at each other. As she pulled in, Dizzy asked, "What is it? Do you recognize it?"

Sheryl explained, "That car looks like the one Keith used to borrow from Nielsen at the bar."

"How often?" asked Dizzy.

"From time to time. Keith didn't have his own. He had easy access because Nielsen didn't use it much."

Dizzy noted, "It looks like it's been here for more than a day. I'll call it in." She wrote down the license but couldn't get a phone connection at the edge of the wilderness. They were definitely on their own.

Into the Woods

They changed into their hiking boots, made sure they had water and food, fastened their backpacks and set out on the trail. They followed arrows and marks blazed on trees and rocks. As they disappeared into the trees, a blue car eased quietly into the parking lot.

They had been hiking for over an hour. Dizzy was having second (or third) thoughts about the advisability of this expedition. There was no sign of Keith or any other living person. If she had some hope of uncovering clues from Sheryl or Larry about Keith or Dan, that hope was dimmed by the distance between them as they walked single file on the trail.

Dizzy struggled along and stumbled over almost every root and rock. She could hear birds chirping and small animals scurrying through the underbrush, but no people. When she was able to catch her breath, she could appreciate the freshness of the air, its faint fragrance of cold water, trees and the absence of carbon emissions. When the trail was shaded in dappled sunlight, it was quite beautiful. But when she faced the sunlight directly she couldn't see in the glare, so she pushed on, hoping for a shadow to filter and sharpen her vision.

She tripped through streams, scrambled up inclines and held onto trees and anything else she could do to try to keep up. Hearing infrequent sounds of indeterminate origin, she would pause and listen intently. Gradually she got the undeniable feeling that she was being watched. Noisily hurrying up the trail to decrease the distance between her and her companions allowed her to drown out surrounding noises and suppress the feeling of being shadowed by something following them.

She plodded along, gradually developing a rhythm, making it easier. Accompanied by the sound of her own breathing, she began to enjoy her surroundings. Listening for suspicious sounds led to listening to the wind, bird calls, and small scampering animals or birds. The trail and the surrounding woods afforded incomparable isolation. Alone with her thoughts, she tried to fathom what had led Keith Gallon to murder his friend Dan. Was his disappearance and apparent flight enough reason to prove that he had committed that brutal act? The murder was brutal and appeared senseless—like the assassination of Jack Parker. Maybe he had committed both murders. If so, it would clear up both murders with the arrest of one perpetrator.

Even with Dizzy's effort, she only caught glimpses of Larry and Sheryl. They disappeared at every turn or incline. Dizzy was now certain she was being watched or followed—not unlike her visits to the area around the construction site murder. She kept touching the top of her holster for reassurance. Suddenly she heard a shriek up ahead—from Sheryl. She flew up the trail, jumping rocks and skirting branches and roots. As she came around the corner, she saw Sheryl sobbing in Larry's arms.

"What happened? Are you all right?"

Larry was holding and comforting Sheryl. He turned to Dizzy, his attention on her drawn gun, "She just had a scare. Jumped a snake in the trail."

Sheryl looked up and shivered. "I've seen bears, skunks, fishers, moose and bobcats up here; they don't bother me. I know it's irrational, but snakes give me the willies."

Dizzy asked, "Was it poisonous? Where is it?"

Larry took the opportunity to sit on a boulder. He took a swig of water and passed it to Sheryl, who had calmed down. "No, it's not poisonous. It was a harmless black northern racer and it took off. The only poisonous snake in the White Mountains is the timber rattlesnake.

They're in hibernation now—for six months. Endangered species—very shy of people."

Dizzy wondered if the snake was the only surprise in store for her.

———

Keith was alone with his thoughts. He couldn't fathom what had happened—to him, to his friends. Random thoughts filled his panic-exhausted dreams and conscious thoughts. What could he have done differently? How much was his fault? Visions of Sheryl wove its way in and out of his thoughts. Maybe it was his surroundings, maybe guilt. He recalled the hike that he often thought of as The Hike. He and Sheryl had gotten lost. Having descended down the slide designated as the upward part of the trail, they discovered that there were no trail markings into the woods. It was already dusk and they had no way to find the trail.

They had to retrace their steps and hope they could resume their direction on the trail. Now in the dark, more than two hours from their car and out of water, they struggled to find their way. When things were looking their bleakest, the trail appeared—almost miraculously. They hugged with joy and relief. Then suddenly, they shared what might have been a long hidden feeling. They kissed. Paused, then kissed again—a long quenching conjoining. Keith began unbuttoning Sheryl's blouse, and she held him. He could hardly breathe when he looked at her—as he had never looked at her before. Simultaneously and hurriedly they began to remove each other's clothes. Simultaneously and hurriedly they touched each other's genitals. The anticipation was almost unbearable.

Suddenly, they heard something in the woods. Something big, crashing through the underbrush. That brought them to their senses. They dressed quickly. Survival overcame lust or whatever it had been. Even with headlamps, this trail was not the place to be when it got really dark. Hurrying in near silence, they hustled out and a couple of hours later they found their car and left. They never spoke of that day, but Keith was sure that it had solidified their friendship. Once in a while, after a couple of drinks, they would look at each other and say, "If it hadn't been for that Sasquatch…."

———〜〜◦◦❍❍❍❍◦◦〜〜———

Detective Dahlia Gillespie was tired and anxious. After about two and a half hours, she was becoming more and more aware that she was way out of her element and beginning to suspect that she had been played. She was fit and worked out regularly. Between self-defense and cross training, she had experienced fatigue, but this was ridiculous. Not knowing where they were nor where they were going, without any support and hearing strange sounds, she was exasperated.

"Hold up!" she bellowed. The shuffling of leaves up ahead stopped as did everything else. Except Dizzy. She pushed herself to catch up, turned a corner and found Larry and Sheryl drinking water and looking at her with curiosity and a touch of fear.

Dizzy stopped, doffed her backpack and regulated her breath. She stared at them. The two hikers looked at each other as though Dizzy had been turned by a full moon into a snarling, growling werewolf.

"Where the hell are we? I want to know everything about where we are, where we're going, and what we can expect when we get there."

Larry and Sheryl took off their packs, sat on big rounded boulders, and motioned to Dizzy to do the same. They each gulped from their bottles. Dizzy thought, "This is as close as I'm going to get to an office meeting today."

Larry went into his backpack, "This," he announced with a ceremonious flourish, "has the answer to all your questions." He held a small thick paperback aloft and declared, "This is the bible."

Sheryl imitated a hallelujah chorus. "Tell it like it is, Brother Larry."

Dizzy was taken off guard by the sudden humor and it relieved some of her anxiety. She leaned forward.

Sheryl said, "That small, good book is the AMC Mountain Guide. Never leave home without it. It contains maps, descriptions, warnings, clues, and all you ever need to find your way into or out of the White Mountains."

"Larry said, "Of course it's all available as an app or online, but reception and batteries can be unreliable on the trail. Luckily for you, I'm going to summarize. We're in the Pemigewasset Wilderness—which isn't as wild as it sounds. You noticed how we've been following the painted blazes on the trees?

Dizzy nodded understanding.

"Well, you may also have noticed that the marks changed colors at one point and for a while they were double marked?"

Dizzy sipped and waited.

"That's because we've gone from one trail to another."

Sheryl said, "But where we're headed is a little less civilized. Owl's Head is the most remote peak over 4,000 feet in the mountain range. Neither Larry nor I have ever been there."

Larry added, "It was a point of pride with Keith who has. He once commented that a person could be lost there forever."

Dizzy asked Sheryl, "What did you mean by less civilized? It's been very pretty, but it's as uncivilized as I want to get."

The hikers looked at each other. Larry said, "Once you get to Owl's Head the trail becomes a path. It's unmarked and unmaintained."

Less than an hour later Larry and Sheryl stopped and held up their hands for Dizzy to stop. There was no particular landmark or change in the terrain that she could see. They had been circling the base of what could only be described as a mountain—seemingly forever. Larry and Sheryl waited patiently for Dizzy to catch up. As she approached them, she heard what sounded like careful human movement in the thick woods. Was she just imagining that the sound was becoming more sentient, more human? The sound stopped when she got close to the others.

Sheryl and Larry turned and pointed to a rocky incline that rose beyond sight. "Here's where the trail ends. Keith should be at the top. There's a single lean-to, an established campfire site in the clearing and he'll be able to hear anyone approaching. If he wants, he can walk to the perimeter and peer down on anyone climbing up."

Dizzy looked up. It looked daunting and impossible to ascend. She pointed, "Is that how we're supposed to go up?"

Sheryl said, "Yes, it's a slide; it will be quicker and maybe easier than bush-whacking our own way."

Before Dizzy could respond, Larry said, "The scree will make it really tough."

"What's a scree?" Dizzy imagined some weird animal or monster.

Larry answered, "Loose small rocks that kind of cascade when you step on them. Like gravel on steroids. It makes the going a little shaky and slow. It also makes a lot of noise. So by the time we get to where we think Keith might be, he could be long gone."

Sheryl added, "Also once we're on that incline, it's all horizon. There's no up or down. No trees, nothing to orient yourself. It's like being weightless. Picture shinnying up the world's biggest telephone pole. The only way to tell if you're on the trail is by following cairns."

Dizzy was beginning to feel as though she had landed in a foreign country or among the Dothraki in another dimension and didn't understand the language, "Okay, I'll bite—what's 'cairns'?"

"Cairns are little piles of rocks that people leave as markers for others," said Larry.

"How will I recognize them?"

They both laughed. "Most of them are very obvious; they're like little pyramids."

Quarry Encounter

As they circumnavigated the base, Dizzy almost became her nickname as she looked up at the vertiginous height of the cone-shaped peak. As she returned her attention to the trail, she saw that Larry and Sheryl were sitting on a couple of large boulders, with their backpacks off. She took off her backpack and sat next to them. They all looked up at the peak. Dizzy noticed what she was absolutely sure was a genuine, bona fide cairn. Watching her recognition, Larry gave her a circle-fingered affirmation, "This is where we start. Eat something, drink some water."

Dizzy was happy to comply. She devoured half her sandwich and couldn't remember when a sandwich had been so satisfying. The water had warmed a little but it also was extraordinarily quenching. After a few minutes of relief, Dizzy asked, "It doesn't look too high. How long will it take?"

"That's because you're not seeing the top," answered Sheryl. "And once you start up, you won't see the sides either. At least an hour."

Sheryl added, "We don't want to get up there in the dark." Sheryl and Larry walked over to what was undeniably a cairn and started up. Dizzy followed. It was slow going, almost tortuous. The horizon surrounded them as they ascended. They felt isolated and they kept getting separated. After experiencing the absence of any reference point—no trees, no forward, and no back—and sliding on the rocks, Dizzy felt what could only be described as despair. She thought that when—and if—she reached the summit, she could never go down again. At least she no longer had the feeling of being watched. Without surrounding woods, there were no sounds to spook her. After what felt like an eternity, they had surmounted the slide and entered into a very thick and hilly wooded area. Dizzy had never seen woods this dense. The trees were stunted because they were at the tree-line, so close together they formed a tapestry. As they walked the path, they smelled burning wood, a campfire. The odor grew stronger and suddenly they saw the embers of a burning fire. They stopped. No one was there. Then they heard a voice—Keith's.

"What do you want?"

Dizzy said, "We want talk to you."

"So talk," the disembodied voice demanded.

"There are lots of questions to be answered."

"Such as?" Keith approached slowly. Then he recognized Sheryl and his brother for the first time and rushed forward; they all hugged. Keith had tears in his eyes as he clapped his brother on the shoulder and kissed Sheryl on the cheek.

Keith turned to Dizzy, waiting for his answer. Dizzy said, "For starters, what do you know about the death of Dan Daniels?"

Keith sat down right where he stood as though he had been blown over. They all looked at each other and understood. He was stunned. Or he was a great actor.

"You can help us solve his murder by coming back with us."

"Dan is dead? Murdered?" Keith blurted out.

Dizzy helped Keith gather up his stuff, and subtly glancing through it. She took out his hunting knife, showed him that she was confiscating it and put it in her belt on the side of her hip.

Keith watched and asked, "Am I under arrest?"

Dizzy answered, "No, you are not under arrest. I'm just following procedures." Keith just looked at her. "You'll get it back when we get home."

They began the descent. The hike down was easier but more treacherous than the hike up. Once they reached flat terrain and began the long trek back, Dizzy asked Keith to slow down to match her pace. She filled him in on what had happened in his absence; he seemed genuinely surprised and saddened by Dan's death. He was obviously shaken. He said that the main reason he had fled was his fear of Dan who he thought had shot at him. Dizzy digested what the ramifications of the fear might be if he was telling the truth.

Suddenly Dizzy heard shrill and unearthly screams—like a gang gone wild in the distance. She searched their faces. They answered almost in unison, "It's hawks—fucking."

Dizzy shook her head not knowing what to believe and continued down the trail while she listened to Sheryl and Larry and Keith updating each other. As they came to a clearing, Larry pointed up at the sky. Sure enough there they were. Over a half dozen hawks doing lazy circles. Their demeanor made Dizzy visualize them enjoying post-coital cigarettes. She was amazed that animal behavior could be so human. Or was it the other way around?

"Hawks mating," the detective repeated as she watched them circling.

The trail had flattened, but they were exhausted and uncomfortable. They all sat down, broke out their last sandwiches, passed around gorp and snacks, and they drank much-needed water. As they rested, the feeling of being watched suddenly returned to Dizzy. She turned to Keith, "I understand why you might have felt wary about Dan, but remind me again—why were you following him?"

Dizzy watched Larry closely out of the corner of her eye as Keith sighed impatiently, "Because I found out that he was seeing Carolyn, and I wanted to know what else was going on. It was what you might call 'morbid curiosity'." He looked nervously at his brother.

Dizzy turned to Larry. "Larry, you don't appear to be surprised that Dan was seeing Carolyn."

Larry looked at Dizzy and considered for a moment, "Nothing surprises me anymore."

Dizzy put her food down and studied Larry, "Are you sure you didn't know about their relationship before today?"

"Maybe I kind of guessed."

"Is it possible that you knew and forgot? With everything that's been going on?"

Larry thought for a second, "I guess maybe Sheryl told me. I don't remember exactly when."

Dizzy looked at Sheryl, who looked surprised. "Sheryl told me that she didn't tell you; we know that Keith didn't tell you." She waited for all that to sink in.

Larry stood up and stretched, "I guess maybe I saw them together."

Dizzy noticed that Sheryl and Keith were staring at Larry with some surprise and anticipation. She asked Larry again when he knew.

Larry was becoming agitated and reached into his backpack, "What difference does it make?"

"How do you feel about Keith and Sheryl knowing and not telling you?" Dizzy asked.

"I don't know. I don't know why they didn't tell me."

Dizzy stood up, "Maybe they were afraid how you would react. Why would that be?"

Larry was holding his backpack with one hand while his other remained in it. I guess they thought I'd be hurt or pissed."

Dizzy looked at Sheryl and Keith for verification. They were staring in near disbelief at Larry. When Dizzy turned her gaze back to Larry, she saw his gun pointed at her.

She forced herself to be calm and carefully told Larry, "Put the gun away, Larry, that's the smart thing to do."

Larry was agitated. It was either fear or rage—or both. "If you think that I can't, or won't shoot, let me assure you that I can and I will. I shot a lazy useless construction asshole from pretty far away, and I shot that cheating friend from pretty far away also—at least the first shot. The second shot was closer; I wanted him to know who did it."

Dizzy tried to deter Larry from making them his next victims. "You won't kill your best friend and brother…."

Larry just stared at them. Dizzy was certain she heard those human sounds close by, but it didn't seem so important now.

Keith looked at his brother with a mixture of bewilderment, sympathy and fear, "Larry, I don't understand."

Larry looked at Keith, "What did you expect me to do? I loved Carolyn. When she didn't want me anymore, when I failed at my marriage, my life turned to hell. I didn't understand the world anymore. Nothing made sense anymore. It was like I had been transported to another planet. Nothing was clear. I tried to make sense out of it. You know what I found?" Larry waited for a brief second. "I discovered that the only feelings that were clear—and not as painful as my sadness and self-pity—were anger and hatred. I even went to a shrink."

His focus and the gun on them never wavered. "Then I realized I could do something about it. I could make my existence a little better. I could eliminate the annoying, stupid things that made my life miserable. Granted they weren't as important as my marriage—or my divorce. That God-damned construction site pissed me off every day. Cost me time. And they didn't care. I made them care. When I shot that fat bastard, it felt great."

The trio of listeners was stunned into silence. Dizzy couldn't tell if Sheryl and Keith were concerned for their own safety or if they should be, but she concentrated on how to extricate them all from the situation. Just then, there was a thud in the surrounding brush. Larry turned and pointed his gun toward it. Dizzy started to go for her gun. Larry turned and pointed his pistol at her, freezing her in mid-motion. "Hold it. Take your gun out slowly with two fingers."

She did.

"Now with your other hand, hold it by the muzzle and throw it easy over here in this bush."

She did.

Larry went on, letting out all that he had held inside for so long. It was a true confession. It must have been difficult to keep it all to himself. "After fixing the construction site, I began to think about my divorce. I realized that it wasn't Carolyn's fault. If we couldn't live together, so be it. But that conniving shyster of hers caused us misery, cost me and my family money—just so he could make more money. I was just casing out his office to check out his habits and the miserable bastard walked in front of my car. That was his mistake."

Dizzy was trying to figure a way out, a way to get the gun away from Larry. Then she heard the distinct sound of what could only be a human being running toward them.

Larry heard it. He pointed the gun in that direction. Dizzy inched closer and began to ease Larry's hunting knife out of her belt.

"Stop!!!" Larry yelled at her, breaking the relative quiet and causing Sheryl to jump back. "Now just like you did with the gun…. No one has to get hurt, but you know…."

Suddenly, a blur burst out of the woods and knocked Larry off his feet. Then Dizzy was on him a split second later. In one fluid movement, she grabbed his pistol hand with both of hers and slung one leg over his throat and the other over his torso, surrounding his arm. She had a well-positioned Judo arm bar on Larry. She pulled his arm and bent it toward his pinky. His hand popped open like a jack-in-the-box, releasing his weapon. At the same time the tackler held him down. She turned to her cohort, "Hi Rob."

After some maneuvering, they cuffed Larry and the five of them headed back down the trail. Rob led the way and Dizzy followed the three friends. It was not a happy crew. Sheryl sobbed off and on. Keith held her as she was about to succumb to hysteria. Larry was silent. Whether he was in the grip of anger or despondency no one could tell.

Dizzy was exhausted and clearly relieved that she had asked Rob to follow them. She had planned for the worst scenario—the three friends might conspire against her. In that case, Dizzy would be woefully outnumbered on the trail. Not to mention that in the woods, she was in their element, not hers.

The contingency plan worked. Rob had performed his part perfectly. Undetected the whole time and quick and resolute when it counted. In fact, Dizzy had been unsure he had been able to follow them, hardly connecting her feeling of being watched with Rob's presence.

They left the trail and Rob and Dizzy took Larry in one car and Keith and Sheryl drove the other back to the city.

Not Quite Out of the Woods

It was the first day of the next month. Julie had called The Patient a couple of times but had not been able to make contact. She looked at the date circled in red. She couldn't imagine what the box contained, so she didn't try. She placed the box on the sofa patients customarily sat or reclined on. She used a utility blade to sever the packaging tape. When she lifted the lid, she found three items inside. The first was a plastic bag; it contained a chess piece—a black king. It was hand-carved in onyx and looked very expensive. She put the bag down gently and picked up the next item. It was an empty Jack Daniel's whiskey bottle. She turned it over and over in her hands, and was mystified. What was so important about an empty liquor bottle?

The third item was lying flat on the bottom of the box, almost like lining or packaging material. When she looked at it closely saw that it was a newspaper front page. She slowly read the headline—*Construction Worker Shot by Sniper*. It was then that she understood. The newspaper was a trophy. The site was the same that The Patient had vandalized. She knew enough about sociopathic behavior to realize that the other two objects probably represented other crimes. She locked her door and called the police.

A week later, Larry had been charged. Since he was likely to be called as a witness, Rob was not the prosecutor. Rob's colleagues would prosecute. Dizzy and Rob went out for drinks to commemorate, rather than celebrate, the conclusion of the case. They met at the Seaport Hotel near the Moakley Federal Courthouse. They arrived at about the same time from different entrances. As they walked toward each other, Rob realized that working with a detective of Dizzy's caliber had enhanced his confidence. For her part, Dizzy was thankful Rob had shown up to rescue her and execute the arrest without real violence. They eased into stools at the long bar, ordered martinis and clicked their glasses. Dizzy toasted, "Here's to finding and stopping a killer."

Rob seconded the toast with, "Here's to finding and starting a beneficial relationship."

Dizzy thought it over and added, "Actually a friendship."

They sipped and thought. "I'm glad it's solved, but it's sad," commented Dizzy.

Rob agreed. "Who would have guessed that both our cases had the same perpetrator? And yet I really don't hate Larry Gallon or fear him."

Dizzy sipped her drink, "I don't know. I've been involved with a number of homicide cases and felonies. Most of them never involved the degree of intent or malice that these cases did."

Rob said, "Was it really 'malice'? Was Larry Gallon really some kind of evil mastermind?"

"Well, he murdered three people in cold blood...."

Rob clarified, "But there was no selfish motive. No greed. No scheme. Just anger."

Dizzy agreed, "In his mind, he was punishing people who deserved it. It was a bizarre take on justice and retribution."

Rob commented, "So his intentions were a kind of biblical justice, sort of 'for the greater good' in his mind?"

Dizzy finished her drink and said, "It gives new meaning to 'The road to hell is paved with good intentions.'"

Before they went their separate ways, they hugged. Each had learned from the other; they had worked well together. Rob said, "It might be nice to work together again." Dizzy smiled the widest smile Rob had seen in a long time.

———

Keith and Sheryl got in Michael Nielsen's car and headed out to visit Larry. As a convicted felon, Larry was sentenced to Cedar Junction, the maximum security prison on the Walpole/Norfolk line. The ride took well over an hour. Each was lost in thought most of the trip. Silence interspersed by music. Attempts at small talk only served to underscore the awkwardness and discomfort they both felt.

Neither had heard a word from Larry in the six weeks following his incarceration. Actually, they had heard the word "No" both times they had tried to arrange a visit. Finally, now almost three month later, they had been contacted by a social worker at the prison requesting that they visit Keith's brother. They each wondered how he would act, how he would look, how he would react.

After pat-downs, security scanners, and signing waiver forms, Sheryl and Keith were escorted into a small meeting room where Larry was waiting. He was seated and stared at the ground. Sheryl noticed that he had lost a little color and a little weight. Keith watched the prisoner warily, looking for clues as to what the state of his brother's spirit might be. They slid back their chairs and the noise echoed from the linoleum to the concrete walls. Sheryl thought she caught a faint whiff of chlorine bleach.

Larry never looked up, his mind somewhere else, apparently unaware of their presence. Sheryl said, "Hi Larry." The next 30 or 40 seconds seemed to take ten minutes.

Suddenly Larry looked up, flashed a big grin, "Hi guys, it's about time you visited."

On the way home, Sheryl and Keith discussed in animated terms how much Larry's attitude had exceeded their expectations. He hadn't lost his sense of humor. Or he had regained it in the intervening months. They discussed books, movies, music, working out, etc. The two visitors hadn't brought up anything of import, but in some ways, the ghost of Dan Daniels was present. The visitors departed, thinking the same thought. They knew they would visit Larry often.

———〜∽◦∾❀❀∾◦∽〜———

Some weeks later, Dizzy wandered by the Bar None. She entered and sat at the bar. Keith was behind the bar, cleaning glasses, looking like he had lost his best friend—his best friend and his brother. However, he smiled at Dizzy and shook her hand.

"How have you been holding up? Dizzy asked.

Keith said, "As well as can be expected. I'm lucky I have good friends for support."

"That's good to hear. I'd like a dry vodka martini with Tito's and a large green olive," Dizzy said, not concerned about the time and kind of hoping for an overpour.

As he went about preparing the cocktail, Keith said, "Sheryl and I have been to visit Larry a couple of times. He seems to be doing OK." He glanced at Sheryl who waved to Dizzy.

"Do you recognize that woman next to her?"

"I do."

"That's Carolyn Johnston, Larry's ex-wife," said Keith, not realizing it was unnecessary. Dizzy either noticed or imagined the sadness in Carolyn's demeanor.

Keith explained, "With so many issues no longer a problem, she visits from time to time." He brought her drink. "It's on the house."

Dizzy acknowledged the gesture and sipped her martini appreciatively. She gazed over at the table where the Devil's Jury sat. Two chairs at the table had been tilted on their front legs, leaning on the edge of the table—saving places for two people who would never come. One had a small bottle of Jack Daniel's in front of it.

Acknowledgements

I would like to thank a lot of people for their special help in developing this novella. I had a lot of help. There were those who offered encouragement and filled in some of the blanks in the writing and publication process: Francie King, Dick Margulies, Tom Waite, Anne George, Hallie Ephron and Elizabeth George.

Others were sources for specific research: Peggy Krippendorf, Denise Woodruff, Detective Sean Brady, and Myron Tupa.

When I think of those who read and reviewed in various stages, it becomes very clear how much their input affected the work. They each read different manuscripts—sometimes very different. Almost in the order that they read: Lyn Kaplan, Steve Forman, Christine Jellow, Jody Shyllberg, Sheila Eppolito, Kim Rubin, Mike Frantz, Ellen Clair Lamb, Dr. Toni Delisi, Marcia Landers, Les Landers, Kim Kane, Ken Steiner, Mandy Kaplan and Hank Shafran who had the arduous task of nit-picking or what others would call editing.

In addition, I'd like to thank Mystery Writers of America, and Ray Daniel, individually and collectively for tips and tolerance and Jody Shyllberg for the cover design.

For more information, visit my website at DSKaplanauthor.com or on Face Book.

The Author

Former teacher, advertising executive, agency founder and periodical publisher and current jazz musician, marketing consultant, hot sauce fan, bourbon aficionado, movie buff, husband, brother, father and grandfather, D.S. Kaplan has enjoyed creating and meeting the characters of his first novel. He looks forward to their further adventures in the next book entitled *Thief Executive Officer.*

The Book

The Devil's Jury is a suspenseful and humorous whodunit.
I hope you enjoy reading it as much as I did writing it.